Blue Lake Christmas Mystery

by

Cynthia Harrison

Blue Lake Series

This is a work of fiction. Names, characters, places, and incidents are either the product of the author's imagination or are used fictitiously, and any resemblance to actual persons living or dead, business establishments, events, or locales, is entirely coincidental.

Blue Lake Christmas Mystery

COPYRIGHT © 2016 by Cynthia Harrison

Cover Art by *Angela Anderson*

The Wild Rose Press, Inc.
PO Box 708
Adams Basin, NY 14410-0708
Visit us at www.thewildrosepress.com

Publishing History
First Mainstream Mystery Edition, 2016
Print ISBN 978-1-5092-1075-6
Digital ISBN 978-1-5092-1076-3

Blue Lake Series
Published in the United States of America

Bob had lit the pair of hurricane lamps
that anchored the greens. A gorgeous bow on a pine wreath hung over the mantel picked up the gold tones on the edge of the pretty plates. Hanging under the mantel were two stockings for the boys, Corky and Sidney. They were of course red to match the tablecloth. Holly could not have created such a tableau herself. It was a work of art. "Bob, everything is so lovely."

"I didn't do it. Eva. My sister-in-law."

"Oh, well, good because I really don't like a man who is a better decorator than I am. But you designed this house, right?" Holly felt a warm glow that Bob would enlist someone to decorate for her. She hadn't given a thought to decking her own rented halls, but now she felt in the mood. "This place is a little jewel."

"Thank you. The condos will be more in this style. Lots of glass for views of wooded areas."

"Oh, the condos! I want one already."

"I'll take you to view the site tomorrow if you like."

"Yes, I would. Is it okay to get my photographer to take pictures to run with the article?"

"Sure. Hey, you want some wine?"

"I'd love a glass."

Bob pulled a bottle out of his fridge and opened it like a pro. "I noticed you drink Chardonnay, so I got a bottle of that and a red." He poured her a glass of the white. "Hope it's okay?"

Holly sipped. "It's great. You don't know how much I needed this night out. You are so sweet."

Praise for Cynthia Harrison

"Cynthia Harrison's heartfelt writings push past the boundaries of the modern romance novel. With humor, honesty, and insight, Harrison tackles a variety of relationship issues. Her books are a delight to read, with well-crafted characters and plots that are sure to keep readers turning the pages."

~Cindy LaFerle,
author of Writing Home
and Michigan Prime columnist

Dedication

For Al,
the guy who keeps me warm all year long.

Stew Pot

Thanksgiving is two days away! Friday's Fish Fry had record attendance, including the first public appearance of Chloe and Luke Anderson's baby girl, LuLu, now six months old. Don't know why they were hiding her as she is a perfect princess. The Huffingtons' grandson was in town with his mother and father from downstate, just in time to celebrate his first birthday. There was a feast of cake. Eddie Fass's niece Holly Fass has moved into Eva Bryman's bungalow at Blue Heaven and will be reporting all the hard news for this paper beginning with the next issue. Her first assignment is covering the opening of the new library designed by hometown architect Bob Bryman. This columnist thinks it is high time the library had a proper building instead of that tiny annex behind the drug store that was little more than a dingy closet. Until next time.

~ R.McG.

Chapter One

Holly Fass had a list of what she knew and what she needed to find out. She sat, secret notebook in hand, in the living room of her rented bungalow, staring out at the cold lake. Frost iced the lawn all the way to the bluff overlooking the beach. She wrote for ten minutes, then set aside her notebook. She would be late if she didn't leave right now.

Holly parked outside the newspaper office, wobbling a bit in her red peep-toe pumps as she exited the car. She was eager to begin her first assignment as a reporter—yesterday had been the paperwork day, today she'd write a story.

A library opening. Not exactly the sensation between the covers of her secret notebook, but a first step toward that long-held dream, the dream that had brought her here, to Blue Lake. She stood in front of the *Tribune*'s large plate-glass window, looking down Main Street. Her beat.

An agent interested in her secret project told her that legitimate field work, like news reporting and a byline, were key to landing a good book deal. It wouldn't hurt that the story she was secretly writing had happened right here in Blue Lake just two summers ago. And that Holly's cousin was directly involved in the horrible events. The agent had called her cousin "top-tier access."

Holly pulled open the heavy glass door of the *Tribune* offices.

"Honey." Rachel, the *Tribune*'s owner, sat at her big wooden desk, her very blonde hair swishing back and forth as she shook her head. "You need to go home and change those shoes."

For a slow second, Holly thought maybe they had a dress code up here in Blue Lake that banned the showing of toes. But it was a beach town. People showed more than toes every day at the lakeshore. Even strutting through town. Not now, in late November. But she'd been here plenty of years during tourist season. So she stood at the front door, inquiring eyes shooting to Ernie, the newspaper's editor. He'd hired her and mentioned nothing about a dress code.

Ernie cleared his throat and said, "You'll be doing a lot of walking on this job, Holly, so you'll want to wear sneakers."

"Be right back," Holly said. She sprinted out to her car and headed east to the bungalow. The pressing problem at the moment: she was five foot even and most of her shoes had at least a two-inch heel. She was a yoga person, didn't own a pair of athletic shoes. Her flat shoes consisted of flip flops, snow boots, rain boots, and clogs, none of which would really work with this skirt. She supposed peep-toes in late November weren't practical. In fact they were silly. Holly hated feeling foolish.

She turned into a long driveway and raced past six pastel cottages shuttered tight for the season. Chilly Lake Huron churned in front of her, spread out like an endless inky blue blanket. Her toes were downright chilled.

Inside the bungalow, she passed the registration counter for the cottage check-ins and flipped the latch on the pocket door to her private quarters. In the spare bedroom, she confronted dozens of boxes as she pulled off her shoes and let them drop. Which box held her clogs? While technically a few inches taller than flats, the clogs were comfortable if not the height of fashion. But clogs would never work with this skirt. Did she have time to change into jeans?

She checked her watch and realized that when she'd timed her day to the minute last night, she'd clocked herself from the newspaper office to the new library, not from Blue Heaven, approximately seven minutes further away. On the third box labeled "shoes," she found her clogs and carried them into her bedroom, digging in the closet for a pair of clean dark-wash jeans. No to the low rise, no to the ripped pair, no to rivets. She grabbed a pair her mom had given her for her birthday she'd never worn. Perfect. She shimmied out of her skirt and decided the blouse would have to do. Thirteen minutes behind schedule, but she could speed a tiny bit through town to the new library's opening and her interview with the architect.

Unfortunately, the town cop wasn't busy and busted her for going eight miles over the limit. She pulled to the shoulder, took deep breaths, lowered window, and spilled the story of her new job, new shoes, clogs, jeans, the library, the architect. The cop checked her license and registration and gave her a ticket, not commenting on her story except to say "slow down."

Easy for him to say. She stuffed the ticket in her purse next to her new recorder. She was officially late for her first assignment. Determined to remain unflustered, she clicked over to cruise control and the exact speed limit as she made her way across town. She passed the newspaper office, the coffee shop, the boutiques and bars, and finally pulled into the parking lot of the new library. She sent a quick text to Ernie, letting him know she was on assignment and would be in after she interviewed the architect.

A small crowd had gathered out front while a middle-aged man spoke at a podium. She saw to her dismay that the wide red ribbon had already been cut and lay listless and forgotten on either side of the glass doors to the building. A student photographer, the paper's intern, busily snapped photos. Holly headed toward him, checking her little notebook for his name. Tyler Pennington. Okay. He could fill her in on what she'd missed.

"Tyler, hi, I'm Holly."

"Hey." He kept shooting for a minute while she waited, feeling sorry she couldn't tap her toes to release some of her pent up energy. Clogs were not ideal for tapping toes. She'd missed the speech. People clapped and herded inside the new library. Finally, Tyler stopped the shutterbugging and glanced down at her. He was at least a foot taller than her, but then so were most people.

Pencil poised, she asked him what she'd missed. He gave a quick recap. She scribbled notes. The guy who had made the speech was the brother of the architect. Daniel Bryman, town benefactor, had loaned Uncle Eddie money for his bar back in the day.

"Why do you think they cut the ribbon before the speech?" Holly asked Tyler. "Wouldn't it be more dramatic if they did the speech, then cut the ribbon just before people went inside?" She and Tyler walked toward the entrance. He shrugged and shot a picture of the sliding doors opening. Maybe sliding doors were a big thing in Blue Lake. Clearly, she had her work cut out for her. Her secret book idea was sure to put Blue Lake on national radar again. But first she had to prove herself by writing sharp copy about a dull event.

Once inside the library, she felt a frisson of hope. While the outside of the building had been nothing special, bricks and mortar, the inside was spacious and sleekly designed with sunlight pouring in from several high, wide windows. The entryway soared two tall stories. She noted the upper floor and winding staircase across from the cathedral-style lobby. She turned around to look back at the entrance.

A group of spectators pointed and made hushed remarks about the mural painted above the front doors. The painting depicted Blue Lake from its earliest days—Native Americans on the side of Lake Huron catching fish—through the first European settlers, to farming and log cabins, to a prosperous logging town with brick houses, giving way to the current quaint downtown with old-style lampposts, ending at a paved road curving into the new library. Holly debated whether to capture the work of art with words in her notebook or recorder. Notebook for the mural description, recorder for quotes she could skillfully, she hoped, elicit from patrons.

Next she asked a few people for their impressions, recording their delight. One man complained about new taxes. His wife elbowed him sharply and told Holly to pay him no mind. Holly smiled and tried to keep her replies brief to people's queries about who she was and where she'd come from. "Holly Fass. New reporter for *Tribune*. Downstate. Pleasedtomeetyou."

She made her way toward Tyler and asked him to point out the architect.

Tyler pointed his hand still holding the camera toward the youngish Bob Bryman, in his twenties like her, talking to Daniel Bryman. The brothers stood at the edge of a seating alcove, set off by upholstered chairs and a sofa. Holly took a deep breath, hoping neither of them had noticed her tardy arrival. She headed over to the men. She'd done most of her homework on Bob Bryman, Daniel's younger brother, the architect. Her interview with him should give her some good quotes.

At her approach, the brothers broke off their discussion and turned politely to face her.

"Hi, I'm Holly Fass, new reporter for the *Tribune*." She extended her hand toward Daniel, who grasped her fingers with enthusiasm. "And you"—she turned her smile onto disappointingly dour Bob Bryman—"are our architect."

To cover his brother's silence and alarming lack of eye contact, Daniel patted her on the back. "Hello and welcome to Blue Lake, Holly. I hope you'll be very happy here. Bob, Holly's renting the bungalow at Blue Heaven."

Right. Holly remembered that the woman who owned Blue Heaven was married to Daniel, so she'd be Bob's sister-in-law. In this town, everyone was related to everyone else in some way. Even she was related to people who lived here.

Bob silently contemplated the floor.

"Is this a good time for an interview about the

library's architecture, Mr. Bryman?"

"Oh, just call him Bob." Daniel again. "No last names needed here in Blue Lake." Bob seemed to be immersed in the study of the marble-like floor. "I'll leave you to it. Again, lovely to meet you, Holly." Daniel walked toward a small knot of people, patting shoulders and glad-handing as he progressed.

"Is this floor actual marble, Bob?" When he failed to look up or answer, she forced herself to remain silent. One. Two. Three.

"What? Oh, it's man-made. Very durable."

Bob was cute with his lanky frame and thick streaky hair, but he lacked presence. He didn't seem to be there in the room with her, but somewhere else. Away.

Still, she was beyond relieved he'd finally managed to speak in the general direction of her recorder, although with a notable lack of spark. She would not put her personality assessment into the article. Might make readers fall asleep, just the suggestion of how uninvolved he was in his surroundings. In her. Not that she thought she was all that, but guys usually paid more attention than Bob. Never mind. Be a professional, Holly!

"I've been admiring the mural. Did a local artist paint that?"

"Er, yes."

"And what is his or her name?"

Bob mumbled a name. She thrust her recorder closer to his face and asked him to spell it. Maybe he was just shy. Some people were like that. Introverted. She felt a wave of sympathy. So this was difficult for him, to be in the spotlight.

"Perhaps you'd give me a tour?" Holly noted that the librarian guided townsfolk on their own tour. She also noted there were no visible books anywhere in her vicinity. Magazines galore here in the seating area and just beyond, metal shelves of DVDs marched clear to the back wall. She tried to look past that to the bones of the structure, which she had gathered during research was important to an architect.

Bob didn't bite, off to Mars again or locked tight inside his own head. Who knew? Holly plunged forward. "We can start right here. I love this reading nook. And the wood panels on the walls. How did you come up with the idea to arch that big window above the mural? And then you combined—plaster is it?—with wood for the walls. Such a beautiful effect."

She may have overwhelmed Bob with her comments, because he went silent again. Holly briefly wondered if she should have gone to dental school. Conducting this interview was like pulling teeth.

Chapter Two

Bob Bryman was a good faker. He could plaster on a smile for the camera and cut a ribbon with the best of them. And he'd gotten through the interview with the too-cheerful rookie reporter. He sat in his doctor's waiting room, early for his appointment but needing to be anywhere but at the library. The new building simply reminded him he was a copycat. When would he again be able to access that part of his brain that had built his glass house on the river? Come up with fresh ideas of his own? Stop longing for Lily?

Well, that's why he was here. No need to hash things over before his appointment. He thought back to the interview with Holly Fass. Eddie and Dr. Fass's niece. He liked Eddie. They were buddies. So he had made an effort with Holly. Mostly he'd talked about his great-grandfather Vance and how the early-twentieth-century architect had made Blue Lake famous with his Craftsman-style homes. Bob said Vance had been the inspiration for the library and that was true. Since graduating with his master's in architecture over a year ago, Bob had finished exactly two buildings. The little glass house on the Sapphire River almost didn't count, as it was his M. Arch. project.

Then when it was clear Bob could not move on after Lily left town, Daniel had commissioned Bob to do the library. A pity project. The two building styles

9

were completely different, but then he felt like a completely different person during each project. He'd had to force the library and drew liberally from Vance's dusty but grand plans for a library to cap the western edge of town. Vance had only been stopped by the Great Depression. But his plans remained, and despite a Great Depression of his own, Bob had used them to get through the project Daniel had commissioned.

Dr. Courtney Fass came out and said hi, ushering him into her inner sanctum.

She asked if he'd like some water. He said no.

"How can I help you, Bob?"

"Eva thought I should see someone." Eva was his sister-in-law, and he loved her as if she had always been part of the family. It was a small family, only Eva, Daniel, him, and now a little baby on the way. Bob wanted to feel better for everyone's sake. "I haven't been able to get over Lily." Blue Lake was a small town, so Dr. Fass knew who Lily was, knew what had happened, was it more than a year ago? Closer to two years. "It's been a long time, and Eva thinks I should be dating again. But I just don't feel like it."

"Have you been in contact with Lily?"

"I was. But she changed her phone number, ah, a few times. So, no, not now."

"Why did she change her number?"

"I, ah, she said—" This was hard. It might have been a mistake to come here. "She said she needed a clean slate. You know, after everything that happened."

Dr. Fass nodded, her face turning just a shade paler.

Bob realized Dr. Fass's daughter had been the young girl Lily had saved from rape. Damn. Dr. Fass was the only therapist in Blue Lake, so what else could he do?

"Is it okay to talk about the case?"

"It's fine, Bob."

"Well, my involvement wasn't really publicized, but I knew about Lily's problems a long time ago. Let's see, I met her the summer we both graduated high school. She came here—well, she was passing through—and I got her a job helping Eva at Blue Heaven. This was before it opened. Lily stayed in one of the cottages. I didn't know why she'd left home, not at the time, but later I found out."

Bob stopped. It was uncomfortable talking to a woman about rape. Especially because her own daughter had almost been raped, and not that long ago.

"Lily was raped by her cousin, the same guy who attempted to rape Ruby, the guy Lily shot and killed, saving Ruby." Dr. Fass said this without being overly emotional about it, considering Ruby was her daughter.

Miserable, Bob nodded. No matter her demeanor, this couldn't be easy for Dr. Fass. "Lily told me about how she was going to get her cousin to confess on tape to killing her mother—"

"She thought her cousin killed her mother?"

"Originally, yes. Then eventually, we found out it was her father. That's about all of it. Well, except we were involved, like—"

"Were you in love?"

"Yes. All that time, since right after high school. Me, not Lily. She only loved me a little bit, maybe, for a while. That was when she wanted me to help her catch her mother's killer." Bob realized that it was possible Lily had never loved him at all. She'd been

11

one mixed-up chick. Why did he still miss her? Still love her?

"Bob, tell me a little bit about your life. I know Daniel raised you."

"Yeah, our parents died in a car accident when he was in college." Bob stayed with that story for a while, filling in details he'd forgotten.

"How did that feel, to grow up without a mother or a father?"

Bob didn't know how to answer. He wondered if it was a trick question. He felt a little numb. Dr. Fass waited for him to say something. He felt sweaty even though it was cold outside. They were calling for snow later today. He had to say something and not about the weather.

"What?" He had forgotten what she'd asked him.

She repeated the question. How did he feel growing up without a mom and dad?

"I don't know."

"You don't remember?"

"I, uh, feelings, well, I'm sure I cried about it. I was young. Daniel is ten years older than I am. So I was, like, eight years old."

"Sad."

"Yes, sure, wouldn't you be?" Bob felt stupid for saying that. She was just trying to help, and here he was getting all defensive. But he really didn't know what having no parents had to do with loving Lily. "Sorry," he said.

"I know it's difficult."

"What?" He meant, what was difficult. He didn't understand what she meant or what she wanted him to say. He felt confused, even more confused than when he'd arrived.

"Can you remember other feelings growing up? About not having parents?"

She was still on the parent thing. He'd have to play along for an hour. He looked around her beige office. A clock and a box of tissues sat on a table with a beige lamp. Sun came in the window from a gauzy shade. He focused on the clock. Had it really only been fifteen minutes? He had, what, another half hour to go? What could he say? How were you supposed to remember how you felt as a kid?

"I don't remember too much about feeling anything. Well, at Christmas, the other kids' parents came to the school play. And my friends all had moms. Some of them made cookies. Like that. So I missed having a mom. I guess I was sad those times. Daniel was a pretty good dad, though. He did baseball with me. Little League. He came to my games in high school. But a mom would have been nice. And a dad too, so Daniel could have finished college."

Dr. Fass wrote in her notebook. She looked up as if expecting him to go on.

"That's about it, really," he said.

"Is there anything about Lily, about your relationship with her, that reminds you of how you felt when you were missing your mom and dad?"

He almost said "What?" again. But he stopped and thought about it. Was there anything? "Well, Lily wasn't with me most of the time. My mom and dad weren't with me, either, so there's that."

Dr. Fass didn't write that down. She nodded. "How do you feel when you think about Lily being away?"

He saw now why there was a full box of tissues

within reach. People probably cried here a lot. Dr. Fass had a way of getting right to the very sad parts. All this talk of feelings. She waited for him to say something. Therapy was hard work. He hoped one session would be enough. "I feel sad."

Dr. Fass didn't have to say *like when you thought about your parents.* Her implication was clear. He wasn't an idiot. He grabbed a tissue and wiped his eyes.

"Yeah."

After he sniffed awhile, she said something that wasn't a question finally.

"Maybe you feel comfortable connecting 'sad' with 'love,' Bob. Not that you like it, but it's familiar. Does that make sense?"

He guessed it did. He was messed up. "Okay, let's say that's true. How do I fix it?" Now he had a goal. He wanted to get better, get over Lily.

"Make new friendships, happy friendships."

"I would, but I can't seem to get interested in anything."

"Do you have friends, Bob?"

"Sure. I mean, I go out with the guys for a beer on Friday night. I'm just not interested in dating anyone."

"Have you thought about it?"

"Yeah, I guess. I mean, I talked to your niece Holly today. She interviewed me about the library. I, uh, Eva told me I should do 'random acts of kindness,' so I pulled this speeding ticket out of Holly's bag. It was sticking out anyway. And I'm going to pay it for her right after this session. Does that count?"

"So you thought about asking Holly out, but you decided to pay her parking ticket instead?"

"Right."

"Now, Bob, think about how you felt when the idea of asking Holly out came up."

Bob thought. The silence grew. He realized he had to share his thoughts. He tried to put them in some kind of order. "Well, I thought she was pretty. And I felt a little vibe, you know, like, hmmm. And then I thought about Lily, and that's when Holly went to get a coffee at the buffet in the auditorium and I saw her purse with the ticket sticking out, so I just took it. I felt relieved after that."

Bob knew he had spoken a mouthful, and he hoped that was enough to satisfy Dr. Fass. She was writing in her notebook again, so he was hopeful.

"Good," Dr. Fass said.

Bob had no idea what was good about it. "I don't see what's good about it," he finally said. "I was relieved not to be asking someone out. How is that good? Unless you're happy I'm not thinking of becoming involved with your niece?"

"Bob, you're a nice young man, the type of young man any family would welcome as a date for an age-appropriate family member. What I meant was it's good you have romantic feelings for someone other than Lily. Then relief. Interest and relief, Bob. Those were your feelings today. What do you suppose that feeling of relief might mean?"

Bob was baffled. It seemed obvious to him. "I was relieved not to have to ask her out because I can't risk it." He couldn't believe he'd blurted that out. Stated so clearly his insecurities about women.

"Because?" Dr. Fass prompted.

"Because so far I have not done so well in that department."

"Okay. Fair enough. How many serious relationships have you had, Bob? Think back to high school, before Lily. Was there anybody special?"

"No. Not really. I dated, but mostly we did a lot of stuff as a group. I never got really close to any one girl in our crowd. I liked a few of them, but no, nothing serious until Lily." Bob was starting to get the feeling this was leading back to his parents again. He really didn't want to go there.

"This was a great start, Bob. We'll pick it up again next week, okay? Meanwhile, I want you to think about what we've discussed. Name the feelings as they come up."

"You're not going to say anything to Holly? That I'm your patient or anything else?"

"No, Bob. That would be unethical. What we say here stays between us."

"Good. Because I'm probably not going to ask her out."

"That's fine."

"I'm going to probably just pay her ticket instead."

Dr. Fass's raised eyebrows alerted his inert brain that something wasn't exactly right. "What?" he asked.

"I'm very pleased that you're reaching out this way. I just wonder if you might have done something a little less…" She hesitated. "What I mean is, what will happen when Holly finds that she's lost her traffic ticket? She may become concerned, which will have the opposite effect of what you hoped to achieve."

Bob was damned if he did and damned if he didn't. Dr. Fass must have sensed his frustration because she took another couple of minutes to go over this random-acts-of-kindness thing with him.

"You might do something like pay for the lunch of the person behind you at the take-out window."

Bob was perplexed. "We don't have a single drive-thru in Blue Lake. And how do I pay for a lunch somebody didn't even order yet?"

"Bob." Dr. Fass smiled kindly. "You don't have to do the acts in Blue Lake, not necessarily. And you can just donate what you feel like giving toward a meal. These gestures don't have to involve great sums of money. Or any money. Just think of ordinary kindnesses you can do for people. Maybe bring an apple to a friend."

Bob thought an apple was a crappy gift. Maybe a pie.

"Even if you sincerely compliment someone. Or send a card in the mail. Rescue a stray."

Bob couldn't imagine having to care for an animal. But he didn't say that to Dr. Fass.

Finally, the session was over. Bob wandered out into the cold, not noticing the wind until it whipped the first snow of the season across his face. He pushed the button to start his car. The phone on the dashboard trilled. His phone did not recognize the incoming caller. Maybe it was Lily ringing with her new cell number.

Bob disconnected, his bashed heart beating painfully. It hadn't been Lily on the phone but some developer wanting to meet to discuss a proposed condo development. Bob was not very interested in it. He hadn't been very interested in work for a while now, but he'd gone ahead and made an appointment with the developer. He dutifully thought about his feelings. When he realized it had not been Lily on the phone, it felt like he was gulping Lake Huron's frozen water.

What could he do? He had to take action. But what? He'd promised Dr. Fass he'd do another act of kindness today. Something small. His mind was a big fat blank.

He went into the police station and paid the parking ticket, then walked back out to his car. Thinking about his feelings was going to be a lot of work. Most of his feelings were unpleasant, and so he tried not to think about them, just to get through them. He needed to focus. On anything. The van next to him. Lettering on the side. The mobile vet unit. Why was it here next to police headquarters and not across the street at the vet clinic? Could he park Mary's mobile unit closer to her office? Would that be a big enough kindness? How would he get her car keys? Never mind. It was just too complicated. Mary had graduated from Blue Lake High with him. They'd never dated, not that he remembered anyway. She wasn't his type. Lily had been his type. He'd met Lily the summer after graduation. He pushed his mind away from Lily. Back to Mary. Mary. Bob had seen her name on an ad at the grocery store saying her office was boarding two dogs needing rescue. Rescue. That had been on Dr. Fass's list of kindnesses.

Bob remembered the ad because it was so unusual to have stray dogs or cats in town. Everyone knew everybody else, and nobody abandoned their family pets. Must have been summer people, which was a damn shame. Bob got out of his car, determined not to think about Lily. He strode across the tiny patch of park to the other side of the square and walked into Mary's office. A receptionist he recognized was typing on a computer. Three older people sat with animal cages from which meows and barks emitted. Bob felt an edge, if not exactly an end, to his gloom. He could do this.

He didn't think. He just acted. "Hi there, Joann. About those two dogs…"

"You want 'em?"

"Yeah. Can I pick them up in a couple of hours?" He was not about to tell Joann that he was doing this as therapy. His therapy dogs, for God's sake. Better than Prozac, he thought. "I need to pick up some supplies."

"We've got everything you need right here," Joann said. She had a big smile on her face. Bob found himself smiling back at her. His grin felt a little rusty from disuse.

"Oh well, that's great!" Bob panicked. He could just say he'd changed his mind and leave. No explanation needed. But he didn't. Instead, he pulled out his wallet to pay for the pile of stuff Joann was assembling.

****

When Holly left the library, it was snowing. She headed toward the town square. This would be her beat, and she'd better get used to pounding the cold pavement digging up stories on a daily basis for the foreseeable future. She parked in front of the police station. She still could not believe she'd lost that traffic ticket. She hoped the cop who had written it would not give her a second one for losing the first.

She pulled herself out of her head, and with deliberate eyes took in her new town, noting official-looking buildings flanking the square. A sweet little park shaded with spruce and pine trees and sprinkled with iron benches perched in the center of the square. The spot was perfect for sipping a coffee while contemplating her next big career move: a true-crime story that would rivet the nation.

She decided her first action after fixing the ticket issue would be to visit the site of the fatal shooting that had saved her cousin's life. Holly could see her LinkedIn profile now. "Award-winning journalist and true-crime author."

She stepped out of her car. The wind picked up; the snow slanted sideways into her eyes. She shivered.

Inside the almost steamy cop shop, a woman sat in front of a Formica countertop separating civilians from police, her head turned away from Holly as she spoke into a black landline. Holly's cop was just beyond her at one of two desks. The other was empty. Holly had a vague impression of offices, or maybe jail cells, off the main room. She'd never been inside a police station before. She stood waiting to be noticed, but nobody paid any attention to her so she called out hello to the cop at the desk. He looked up from his newspaper and slowly got to his feet.

"Well hello, Holly Fass, cub reporter."

Smart ass. She hid her disdain as he ambled slowly over to where she stood. Somehow blue-eyed blonds with big shoulders always thought they were hot shit. Holly concentrated on not shaking her head in disgust. She needed something from this guy, this Officer Sam Carpenter. She hadn't noticed his name badge when he'd pulled her over, which made her a little mad at herself. She was supposed to observe everything. Her job depended on it.

"Hello again," she said as sweetly as possible. "I am so sorry, but that ticket you gave me this morning seems to have gone missing. I had it in my purse, and it just vanished while I was at the library covering the opening." He grinned so wide and smug she wanted to smack him. She didn't have anything against cops, but this one rubbed her way wrong. "Could you maybe write it again? So I can pay it?"

"Not necessary," the woman, now off the phone, said, coming over with her hand held out. "Nice to meet you, Holly. I'm Amanda, the dispatcher. Sam, why don't you go back to reading your newspaper? I'll fill in Holly here." Holly shook the proffered hand, thankful that "Sam" did as he was told. Maybe Amanda was his mama. The age difference seemed about right. So did Amanda's tone of voice.

"So the ticket has been paid," Amanda said.

"What? How? By who?"

"Well, the gentleman would like to remain anonymous," Amanda said.

Sam snorted over his newspaper, which Holly noted was not the *Tribune* but the *Detroit Free Press*. Was Sam new in town, too? Did he come from downstate like her? She'd certainly come to Amanda, not Sam, for anything new on the police blotter.

"Everyone here is so kind." Bit of an exaggeration with Sam and Bob, but she wanted to play nice with Amanda.

"Well, Sam here shouldn't have gone and given you a ticket. I heard he made you late to your first assignment. Only eight over the limit and nobody crowding the town now that tourist season's done." Holly smelled a potential font of information as sure as she smelled burnt coffee with an overlay of sugar.

Holly lowered her voice and leaned in closer to Amanda. "I appreciate you saying that, Amanda. Is Sam by any chance new here?"

Amanda nodded. "It was just Harlan and me until

they brought in Sam after the Trouble."

Holly's heart picked up speed. "I heard about that. Lily Van Slyke, right?"

Amanda nodded. "First killing in this town, and I hope the last. We had all sorts here. *People* magazine, network TV reporters, cable folks from Fox news."

"Do you know where Lily is now?"

Amanda shook her head. "Nobody does." Then she leaned over and whispered,

"Bob Bryman paid your ticket."

Bob? Really?

"Looks like he's finally coming out of his funk," Amanda said. "He's been bent out of shape forever over Lily."

The new information burned itself into Holly's brain. She could probably write a chapter now. The agent had wanted to see a revised proposal and three chapters before offering Holly a contract. Maybe she'd just clarify her facts with Amanda. "Bob was involved, like"—she lowered her voice since Sam seemed to be interested in what she was saying all of the sudden— "like they were dating?"

Amanda nodded, casting a look at the phone as it spit out a jarring ringtone. "Gotta go, but you're all set, hon. Welcome to town!"

Holly didn't bother saying good-bye to Sam. It was time to get back to the office and glean further details about her gloomy shining knight, Bob Bryman. Well, at least now she knew why he was gloomy.

Chapter Three

Holly walked along Main Street to the hair salon. The Farmer's Market had set up for Thanksgiving behind the Lion's Club building. Lots of people her age looked on as little kids ran around the pumpkin patch. People here her age with kids? Maybe she'd make some friends. Even if they came with kids, which really was not anywhere on Holly's agenda. Raising a family in your twenties was fine, but she had an altogether different plan. Starter job at small-town newspaper leads to big career as a true-crime author.

She pushed open the door of the salon. Heads in various states of foil and curlers sprouted from pink capes. Someone in the spa area indulged in a mani pedi. Holly didn't get that; she painted her own nails. Piece of cake. Plus you didn't have to go out in the snow wearing flip flops.

The receptionist looked young, still in high school, like Tyler Pennington. Holly texted Tyler and asked if he could get shots of the kids in the pumpkin patch. Tomorrow's vague assignment was "Blue Lake Prepares for Thanksgiving." Ernie said it would give her a feel for the town. Tyler didn't text her back. Fine. She looked up from her phone. The receptionist stared at her, a frown punctuating her forehead.

"Hi." Holly smiled and introduced herself. "My employer, Rachel McGraw, is meeting me here. She said you give great haircut." So far today, Rachel had insisted on changing Holly's footwear, her coffee flavor, and now her hair. Next, she'd probably invite Holly to join the country club where she'd decided they'd have dinner to cap off Holly's "first story celebration." Holly was relieved that Rachel was retiring tomorrow. She did not need a Momager.

"Yes, right. You'll be with Ted." The receptionist relaxed and led Holly through the salon.

Holly had always had long hair. All she'd ever done was a trim. She didn't even have bangs. Her hair was so long she had to stand up so the stylist could cut the ends. But somehow Rachel had persuaded her that it was time for a change. Rachel had even suggested a bob. Holly was not going to get a bob. Although she'd like to interview Bob about Lily. Meanwhile, maybe she could persuade Rachel to spill a few book-worthy details over dinner.

"Do you know what you're having done? Any highlights?"

Holly liked her dark hair. "No, but maybe some bangs? Layers?"

"Drastic!" the girl said in an approving tone. "Here's Ted." Holly said hi to Ted and sat in the chair he swiveled toward her.

An hour later, Holly examined her new hair. She loved it. So shiny and swingy. Rachel had her hair done too, but it looked exactly the same as it had this morning.

"I'll drive," Rachel said. "Back roads."

It had started snowing again, so Holly was happy to be a passenger. "I guess the biggest story the *Trib* ever published was the one about my cousin," she said to Rachel. "And the woman who saved her."

"Lily saved Ruby," Rachel said. "What a mess, poor thing. Lily had a tragic life." Rachel barely let a breath escape between sentences. "Now don't you worry about getting a big story. This is a quiet town, and we like it that way."

"Yes, ma'am." Holly felt she was being reprimanded.

"What's this ma'am nonsense? I'm Rachel." A quick breath. "Now...I heard you talking to Ted about what to do on weekends. You know, my daughter has been invited to join some social club. Maybe—Well, here we are!" Rachel parked the car.

Rachel stopped talking as they navigated the slick walkway. The country club was on the lake, and they were shown to a table with a view. For a Tuesday night, the place was busy.

"Everyone's celebrating the new library!" Rachel said. "Hi, sweetheart."

Rachel's daughter was already seated, waiting for them.

Rachel introduced Holly, then said, "Colette, what's the name of that club you joined?"

"The Fun Divorce Club," Colette said, rolling her eyes.

"Obviously not for you, Holly," Rachel said.

****

Although she'd been like a mother to him while he was growing up, Bob really didn't want to go to Rachel's retirement party. He did not like socializing, except with the guys on Friday night. He liked it here, with his dogs, in his house on the river.

He took the dogs outside and threw sticks for them

to fetch in the snow. Sidney, the lab mix, was an old pro. He fetched and fetched while Corky the corgi raced after Sidney's tail as fast as his short little legs would carry him, stumbling and tumbling in the snow.

Bob's mood changed after fresh air and exercise. He was good to go for Rachel's big night.

By the time Bob arrived in town, it was dark and the party had spilled outside the *Tribune* building. Everywhere Bob looked, lights twinkled. Swags of evergreen topped with big red bows draped lamp posts. A guy in a top hat and long coat roasted chestnuts over a blazing barrel of fire. Not his crowd, but that was fine. Bob ambled down a few doors to Sanchez's place, surprised to see it lit up. Bob went inside.

"You open off season now?" Bob asked the Mexican restaurateur, who stood at the door, greeting customers.

"Naw, just tonight for Rachel. Ernie's having the buffet here after champagne in the office."

"Guess I'll start early then," Bob said heading toward the bar.

He called Rachel to tell her he was at Sanchez's. "Your popularity makes it impossible to get in the door of the *Trib*," he said.

Rachel said she'd be down soon. "Holly…" she called out before Bob could hang up the phone.

Holly. Of course she'd be with Rachel. She was the new reporter. He'd read her piece on the library online. She'd quoted him.

"What can I get you?" The bartender looked familiar, but then just about everybody in town did. Especially off-season.

"Corona," Bob said. Servers were setting out a

buffet. He was hungry. He'd fed the dogs but hadn't eaten himself since breakfast. He helped himself to chips and salsa on the bar.

Holly blew in on a gust of snowy wind, her hair under a blue knit cap that matched her eyes. "Hi Bob," she said.

"Hi."

She ordered a margarita on the rocks and turned to him. "Thank you," she said.

Bob sipped his beer. "For what?"

"Paying my ticket." She pulled off her hat and ran her fingers through her shaggy hair.

"Amanda has a big mouth."

"A reporter's dream." She sipped her drink. "Rachel asked me to hold the table. She wants you to join us."

"Oh. Okay." Bob got up and followed Holly over to a large round table. He wondered who else would be sitting with them. He took a seat next to Holly but told himself it was because he thought it would seem odd if he sat anywhere else. Something was different about her. Hadn't she had long hair the last time he'd seen her? "Your hair looks nice," he said.

"Thanks." She glowed a little bit, pleased.

Dr. Fass would be proud of him. He was getting the hang of this kindness crap. Well, it wasn't crap, not really. People seemed to like it. He was just being a decent person, that was all.

"I think Rachel might be trying to fix us up," she said.

Bob had no idea how to answer that, so he took a long pull from his beer. He'd almost finished it. A server came by with another. He crunched a chip loaded with salsa.

"Well, don't worry. Amanda told me your heart is already taken."

Holly did not talk like a normal girl. She was very vocal. Was that because she was a reporter? If he had to put feelings to it, as Dr. Fass would be sure to ask, he thought she made him *feel* confused but also alert, warm but then chilled. He didn't like any of it. Well, maybe he liked feeling alert. And warm.

He changed the subject. "So how do you like Blue Lake?"

"So far, so good," she said, then, "So you like Mexican food?" Holly handed the empty chip bowl to a server and asked for a refill.

He'd inhaled it all. "Haha," he said. "Forgot to eat today."

"I'm really impressed by this town," Holly said. "I did the square yesterday, and today I checked out the businesses on the strip."

"It's great that they're able to stay open until after the holidays. Everybody used to close up shop come September."

"Really? Where did kids buy school clothes?"

"Target over in Richland."

"Why doesn't Blue Lake have a Target? Hey, I'm sorry. I don't mean to be interviewing you again," Holly said.

Bob laughed. "Nice article," he said. "Read it online."

"Thanks," Holly said, looking down and stirring her drink.

Damn. That was the second time he complimented her. Well, he wouldn't feel too bad about it. He didn't want to have to report on his feelings about Holly to her aunt. If his feelings were neutral, just ordinary kindness, there would be nothing to discuss. "We have an ordinance about chain restaurants and chain retail. Nobody wants 'em. People here have to make a living, and small businesses are the way they do it."

"It adds to the charm," Holly said.

Then Rachel came in with her entourage, and that new cop, Sam Carpenter, sat down on the other side of Holly. Good. She could be cute and charming to Sam now. But after ten minutes of mostly listening to Sam, Holly turned back to him. "Where do young single people live around here?"

"I live in a house, but there's not a lot of choice. No apartments or condos. Well, not yet." Bob thought about the development he'd agreed to design. "Soon," he said.

"What do you know? What have you heard?" Holly sure had a nose for news.

"Well, it's too soon to put this in the paper, but I just inked a deal with a development company that wants to do a project out in Blue Lake Woods, just west of town."

"What kind of development?"

"Condos and apartments. Short-term leases for summer people."

"Wow, see I need somewhere to live when tourist season starts."

"They won't be ready in six months."

"Will they be expensive?"

Bob didn't know how much reporters earned. Probably not a lot. He just shrugged.

"When can I break the story? Can I quote you? Do

you have background information I can print?"

Bob started in on his third beer. He was going to need it to deal with all these feelings. Somehow, Holly made him feel alive and even interested again in his career.

Chapter Four

Before she left her aunt and uncle's dining room, Holly was determined to bring up her true-crime idea. Rachel and Bob had both kept their lips zipped when she'd brought up the topic. Plus, it was only fair to tell her relatives, since Ruby had been a big part of the story. Her cousin seemed fine, like a normal teenager, scarfing Thanksgiving dinner and excusing herself before the pumpkin pie.

Well, it hadn't been the right time during turkey. Or mashed potatoes. Or cranberry sauce. Maybe over pie? Now that Ruby had left the table? Holly choked just a little bit on a wedge of pie crust. "It's so good I'm eating way too fast," she said.

"There's plenty more," Uncle Eddie said. Aunt Courtney started cutting Holly another piece.

"No, really, I can't. I am so full, but thanks, Aunt Courtney."

"Glad you enjoyed it, honey."

Okay. She finished her pie. Now was the time. Aunt Courtney started cleaning up, stacking dishes for the kitchen. Now or never.

"I need to talk to you guys."

Aunt Courtney placed the dessert plates back on the table and sat down again, all attention. "What is it, honey?"

"I, uh, my goal in moving here was not just to get a

31

job on the paper. It's a good first step, but I'm writing a book, too."

"That's wonderful!" Aunt Courtney said.

"What kind of book?" Uncle Eddie asked.

"A true-crime book about Lily Van Slyke."

Aunt Courtney's eyes filled. Oh no. Uncle Eddie's face could be on Mount Rushmore. Holly felt funny, like she was too warm, like she might faint. She had to think. "I'm not putting in anything about Ruby!" Why had she ever thought it had been a good idea to include her cousin in the story? Sweet Ruby who had been through so much.

"Even if Ruby isn't in the book, she's part of the story." Uncle Eddie got up from the table, his napkin floating to the floor.

Holly seemed to be the only one who noticed. Aunt Courtney wasn't looking at her but tracing the pattern of the tablecloth with her finger and blinking back tears. "He's right," she finally said, smoothing the linen and rising as well.

Holly bolted upright as Aunt Courtney reached for the china. Holly was the only one still sitting down, and she felt weird. She took her napkin off her lap and folded it on the tablecloth.

"It will be okay, you'll see." Holly revised in her head. "It's about Lily's family and how they betrayed her and how she rose above it. Blue Lake isn't even in the book at all!" Crap. She'd wanted Blue Lake in the book. The town had been a catalyst for Lily's courage. Never mind. She'd figure it out later.

"Lily won't thank you for writing about her," Aunt Courtney said.

"Of course I'm going to get her permission first!"

Holly hadn't even thought about asking permission. She had no idea how to contact Lily. Nobody knew where she'd gone. Well, maybe Bob did. Would he tell her? She'd have to ask him, then he'd want to know why, then she'd have to tell him about the book.

"And if Lily says no, then you'll drop this idea?" Uncle Eddie waited for her reply.

Aunt Courtney silently carried the dishes into the kitchen. Holly heard a clatter of china and cutlery. Water running. Pots and pans banging.

"Yes," she answered Uncle Eddie. "But this agent I'm in talks with says plenty of people write unauthorized books."

"Well, we're just glad you won't be one of them." Uncle Eddie came around the table and touched her shoulder. "You're a good girl, Holly. Aunt Courtney packed leftovers for you."

****

Holly wasn't a good girl. She was a frustrated woman. On so many levels. But she had a job and a place to stay, at least until tourist season. She checked her speed and slowed as she went through town. Sam had acted very friendly last night at Rachel's retirement party, but she still didn't trust him, even after he'd asked for her phone number. Apparently, Sam couldn't get into the Fun Divorce Club either.

Her phone rang, and for one second Holly thought she'd conjured a call from Sam, but no, it was Rachel.

"Holly! Where are you?"

"Driving. Why?"

"Call me when you get there."

"What's wrong? Wait, I'm pulling in the driveway now." Holly parked and went into the house, dropping her coat on the kitchen table. "What is it, Rachel?" Rachel sounded stressed. Holly hoped she hadn't done anything wrong.

"Ernie's had a heart attack. He's having surgery in Petoskey. I have to go up there. Can you handle the paper? Put something online about him?"

"Of course." Rachel had given her office keys on her first day. "I'm so sorry, Rachel. Is he going to be okay?" From the little Holly knew about Rachel and Ernie, they were old friends whose relationship had warmed through the years into something more. Almost. Or not. It wasn't exactly clear to her what the exact nature of the friendship was, only that it was deep and abiding.

"Eventually, but for a while you'll be on your own. Listen, I have to go. Call me if you need anything."

"Don't worry. I have it covered."

"Thanks, dear."

Holly had been on the job three whole days. She hung up and opened a bottle of wine. Even if she wanted to after the tension at her aunt and uncle's house, there was no way she would be writing her true-crime book anytime soon. The thought was so depressing she drank her white wine warm. Then the agent texted her, asking for a progress report. Holly could probably buy a condo if she had an advance on a book deal. She poured another glass of wine.

****

Holly got through the crazy day working on her own and not knowing half what she was doing by promising herself she would work on her true-crime book for an hour every night when she got home, no matter what. She thought she had enough information to block out three chapters for the agent. She could call Lily about it anytime. She didn't have to ask for her blessing before she'd even signed a contract. But the minute Holly picked up her notebook, the phone rang. Colette. They'd exchanged numbers the other night at dinner.

"Hi, Colette."

"Someone died," Colette whispered. "Come now," she said, rattling off an address. Then she hung up the phone before Holly could ask anything else. Holly looked at her phone. Was this a joke? She didn't think so. And it certainly couldn't be Ernie, as he was in Petosky in the hospital. The address Colette had given Holly was just down the beach. Holly put on her snow boots and grabbed her coat. Her recorder and pad were already in her capacious bag. She slung it over her shoulder and headed out to Lakeshore Drive. The house was a short walk.

Holly arrived at the scene before the police. She came up to Will Hudson's palatial home from the shore, climbing the steps to see the house lit from within, the trees aglow with twinkle lights. All looked peaceful and calm. She felt anything but calm as she approached the house. The great room was empty, and she saw few signs of life in the kitchen. She went around to the street side of the house. Colette was waiting for her. Holly smelled cigarette smoke in the cold night air.

"Oh, thank you," Colette's teeth chattered. "You have to cover this for the paper, but it's hard. Jordan—come here." Colette pulled Holly into the house through a side door. A catering truck had its back doors open, and Holly got a glimpse of steel shelves as she was pulled into the warm air of the house. She smelled bloody beef and heard the whispers of several people in sparkly holiday attire. There were two people in white uniforms, the caterers. When Holly came into the kitchen, everyone parted, and her vision telescoped into the dining room. A man in a tuxedo slumped over his beef, his arms dangling at his sides.

Colette came up next to her and gripped Holly's arm hard, but Holly barely felt it. She'd never seen a dead person before. It took a minute to register that Colette held her so tightly it was painful. She'd have a ring of bruising on her upper arm tomorrow.

"I was sitting next to him," Colette said, pointing at the empty seat beside the inert man, whose body was slowly following gravity despite the chair that had been pushed against him when Colette had jumped from her seat. "One minute we were talking and the next Jordan kind of gasped for air and then just keeled over."

Holly assessed the situation. It looked like they'd barely begun the main course from the full white plates around the gold-clothed table. She smelled rare prime rib and something else not so pleasant. She walked around the abandoned table to get a front view of the body and saw that Jordan had vomited on his plate. That would explain the other odor. His face was twisted in a grimace of intense pain. Frozen that way, in death.

Gradually, the murmur of voices from the party guests clarified into words.

"What's she doing here?"

"Who is that, Colette?"

"She's the new reporter."

"Don't touch the body!" That last was from a voice Holly recognized. Sam Carpenter. The police had arrived.

Four hours later, Holly was allowed to leave 16 Lakeshore Drive and walk home. She had filled her notebook in those four hours despite a caution from Sam and the chief that she should not print speculation, as if she didn't know better than to do that in a newspaper.

"Any cause of death?" Holly was pretty sure what his answer would be, but you never knew. Maybe he could tell by the deceased's upchuck what had happened.

"Unknown," Sam said.

The way his eyes shifted away from her when he said it, she didn't believe him. He knew something. And she needed to talk to Colette. It was going to be a very long night. Once outside, Colette agreed to come to the *Tribune* office so Holly could interview her. Holly got in the passenger seat, although she didn't ask any questions until they got downtown.

Holly pulled out her keys and let them in.

"You've been here what? Less than a week?"

"Correct."

"You're doing a great job."

Holly didn't reply. She was doing fine with the reporting part of the job, but the business end of things was on hold. It was the only way she could cope. Especially with a death to report.

Colette made a pot of coffee while Holly started transcribing her notes for a short fact-based story she could publish in the online edition. Once that was done, Colette took Ernie's desk and Holly sat in Rachel's facing Colette.

"Did you get a story online?"

"Yeah. But I need background for the print edition.

It'll have to be a bigger story."

"No, sure, that's fine." Colette's face was white, and her eyes were tired.

"Was this the Fun Divorce Club party you mentioned the other night at dinner?"

"Yeah. I almost didn't go. Mom's in Petosky with Ernie, and I almost stayed home with the kids. But the neighbor said she'd be happy to babysit, and I've known her forever, so I went. Now I kind of wish I hadn't."

Holly could relate to that. "What about your kids now?"

"I called Mom's neighbor. I explained what happened. She's going to stay."

"Did you call your mom?"

"Yeah. Everything took so long at William's place."

"Is Ernie okay?"

"He's fine. Mom says you'll do a good job. She says you're an excellent reporter."

"Oh, well." Holly wondered if she should have let Colette read the short article before she sent it to the web guy who would upload it to the paper's web edition. "Why don't you start at the beginning. Just take me through it. You drove up to the house…"

"I pulled into William's driveway as another car pulled out. I wondered if someone was leaving the party early. I thought maybe this Fun Divorce Club wasn't so fun after all."

The two of them laughed at that. "Probably just a flower delivery or something," Holly said. "So was it weird to see kids from high school again? What was that like?"

Colette thought about it. "William was the leader of the fun, popular crowd. His status had been far above mine. Class president, football captain, Homecoming king. Every girl in her class of 2001 had a crush on him."

Holly wondered if that included Colette, but she didn't say so.

"Okay, so you're at the door. You knock. What was that first look at William again after all those years like?"

"I admit, I wondered how Will had held up. Was his hair thinning? Did he have a beer gut? I might have been more prepared had I come back for our ten-year reunion, but I didn't. Reunions were so not my thing."

"Mine either," Holly said, having recently turned down an invite to her fifth high school reunion. It was stupid to have a reunion a mere five years after you just got rid of all that high school crap. "Okay, so William was popular, you weren't. What were you like?"

"Awkward. Thick glasses and frizzy hair. I had braces until eighth grade."

Holly had a zillion more questions. You never knew what tiny detail would make a story come alive. "Okay, so then, he answers the door, and what did you see? Give me the interaction, play-by-play."

"Will opened the door. His face was blank. He didn't remember me!" Colette sounded embarrassed. "So to cover the total erasure of myself from his mind in the past ten years, I said, 'Hi, Will! It's Colette!' with that sucky forced seasonal cheer everyone uses this time of year."

Holly let her recorder get the story. It was an interesting story, human interest. But it really wasn't hard news. It was chat, gossip, words that helped Holly learn more about Colette. People fascinated Holly. They were so complex. Everyone had a story. Everyone was the star of their own show.

"I'd brought a bottle of Mom's champagne," Colette went on, "which I shoved at him. I felt suddenly like a little girl dressed up in Mommy's clothes. I mean, I had my own dress on, but I was wearing my mom's winter coat. I really need to get my life together." Colette sighed. She was a good storyteller. And her story made Holly like her. They could be friends. God knows she could use a few. Even though Holly knew the ending to Colette's story, she was interested in how Colette would describe what had happened before Jordan died, really from the first minute she arrived at the party.

"So, then, Will got a load of you, gorgeous and successful and back in town, and he, what? Melted in a puddle at your feet? Asked for your number?"

"Ha. Nothing like. His face went from puzzled to, I'm guessing, feigned recognition. He said 'Hi, Colette! Come in and say hello to everybody.' "

"I saw him, of course," Holly said. "Those cops kept us there long enough. But what about you? Before Jordan died? How did you feel when you saw Will?"

"Well, he hadn't gotten fat, and he wasn't bald. He was as good-looking and muscled as ever and taller than I remembered."

Holly could tell there was more Colette wasn't saying. "How did it make you feel?"

Colette only hesitated for a second before she spilled. "My heart was shooting off nervous sparks, which I ignored, and I said hello to the people scattered around the great room."

"Did you recognize anybody from high school?"

"India and Phoebe and Jordan. India and Phoebe were friends of mine back in the day. Nobody else looked familiar, but then I had not looked familiar to Will. India recognized me right away, though."

"So what's going through your mind?"

"We never have fires in Florida, so at first I was mesmerized by the giant fire burning in a walk-in-sized fireplace. Everything about Will and his house was bigger than I'd expected. Not that I'd had any expectations. Except someone would say exactly what Jordan did: 'Wow how the nerd has turned.' "

"Thinks he's a comedian." Holly said it before she remembered Jordan was now dead. She tucked away that piece of knowledge. That maybe Jordan was not such a nice guy, that he could be snarky. "So what did everyone do when he said that?"

"Phoebe giggled. India didn't. The others looked unsure."

Holly got chills thinking maybe the last thing Jordan had ever said to Colette had been a back-handed compliment. We never know what ignoble gesture we'll be in the middle of when our time is up.

"So what was the food like? The drinks? Was Will a good host?"

"There were a few appetizers sitting around on pretty plates. I was too nervous to eat. Will fixed me a drink—some kind of punch with cranberries in it— everyone crowded onto sofas and chairs next to the fire and looked at me expectantly. 'Let's tell our stories first, so Colette knows how it goes,' Will suggested. Honestly, I like hearing about other people, but talking about myself, not so much."

"Yeah." Holly thought Colette was doing a bang-up job just now. She was painting a vivid picture.

"One by one, like at an AA meeting, they spoke. Name. Class. Number of kids. Years divorced. If they'd left Blue Lake and returned, like me, or if they'd stayed. Jordan, Quinn, and Patrick had left. Typical. All the men. They'd been a year ahead or a year behind me in school. None of them had custody of their kids. Everyone was giving names of kids and ages too, but I'd never remember all that without whipping out my phone and taking notes. Which I was not about to do. Another woman, Kelly, had never left Blue Lake. Kelly was the oldest of the group. I was wondering if she could be the same Kelly my mother had talked about as being the youngest of her group? I felt like it might be rude to ask. But Kelly beat me to it. 'I'm y'all's den mother. My kids are grown, well, in college anyway…'

"They obviously all knew each other's stories, so everyone was directing all their comments to me."

"So that was a nice little respite for you. To just listen. Am I right?"

"Yeah, it was. But then finally I had to give my own little capsule bio. I kept it super short. Everyone raised a glass at the end of my speech. 'Welcome,' Will said, like the Lord of the Manor. I was so nervous, I downed my drink in two gulps. Will asked if I'd like another.

" 'I can get it.' I told him and went to the bar set up on his grand piano on the far side of the room. He followed me. I thought it was weird that he had a bar on such a nice piano, but what do I know about the super-rich? I asked him if he played. It was a dumb question, but it was all I could think to say."

"Did Will seem interested in you? Like a man is interested in a woman?"

"Funny you mention that. Will had been totally checking out my ass. It was so obvious. I remember hoping I wasn't blushing. I remember thinking he was probably still the same. Still racking up points as a ladies' man. Nobody had said why they divorced—Kelly had come the closest in expressing dissatisfaction of long standing—but I was willing to bet Will had cheated on his wife. A bunch of times. And he was probably thinking of a way to add me to his collection. Maybe even as a one-night stand. God, he was so transparent."

"Did he say anything suggestive?"

"No, not really. But he did say something weird. A weird lie I caught him in later."

"Okay, very interesting."

"It started out no big deal. Something like 'Usually we just have a lot of appetizers, but because it's our holiday kick off, we're having a sit down dinner at eight. Hope you're hungry. I've got a prime rib in the oven.' "

Innocuous. Holly quirked an eyebrow at Colette.

"It was the way he said it. Like he was implying he cooked the prime rib. I said something like 'You're cooking for us?' When he said yes I was so surprised I almost dropped my cup into the punch bowl."

"Was the punch strong? Did it have a distinct flavor?"

"It was strong. Tasted more like, I don't know, not like juice. Not like any liquor I've had before."

Holly wrote down the bit about the punch.

"And true to form, Will just had to bring up cooking again. 'Does that surprise you?' he asked. I had no idea what he meant. 'That I can cook,' he said."

Colette got up and poured another cup of coffee. "Want one?" she asked Holly. Holly liked the coffee at Perk a lot better, but she needed to stay awake so she said yes. She didn't want to lose the thread here.

"He was asking if I was surprised that he cooked." Colette reminded Holly. "So I said, yeah, actually I was. And I hate it when people answer a question with another question. Don't you?"

Holly nodded. "Yeah, it's like they're trying to avoid an honest reply."

"Exactly. And typical of what I'd gleaned so far about Will's personality. Are you sure I'm not giving you too much detail? Honestly, it feels exhaustive."

"Nope. You're doing great. You never know when some little thing might turn out to be important later."

"Well, okay. If you're sure. Then I think I decided I shouldn't be so hasty to judge. I was thinking maybe I was a little nervous was all. Tonight was my first venture out as a single woman. Most of my energy since we've moved back here has gone into the children and getting them though the divorce, not to mention shoring up my own battered ego.

"Will was still paying too much attention to me. He needed to mingle with his other guests, but he kind of hovered. I had no idea what to say to him. I was back in high school for that one moment in time, you know?"

Holly didn't know, but she could imagine. She shuddered.

"I thought about how to politely say that I had not expected a former jock to put on an apron. 'I don't really know much about you,' I said, 'just that you played football in high school.'

"He seemed to enjoy that I was a little tongue-tied, like I really didn't know what to say to him. Kelly came up and rescued me, and Will excused himself to see to dinner. Kelly linked arms with me. She's super friendly. She says, 'Will was in your class.' Not a question, a statement. 'Yep,' I told her. 'I've heard stories about him in his heyday,' she says. 'He looks the same, only a little better,' I admitted. We laughed. She said, 'I know how thrilled your mom is to have you back in town.' And I said, 'Mom doesn't like it that the kids are products of divorce.' Kelly said, 'Well, nobody likes that, but it's the reality. We just get on with it. This group helps. Honest.'

"That's about it, really. I took another swallow of the strong punch. Then Will called everyone in to dinner. He had little cards with our names at our places. I was next to Jordan. We sat down, and the Two Sisters began serving dinner and pouring wine. I just had a sip of wine when Jordan slumped over."

"Did you see if he'd had any wine? Or a bite of his dinner?"

"You know what? I didn't notice. I don't think so, though. I mean, I had one sip of wine and no food. But it's possible, I guess." Colette yawned despite all the coffee they'd consumed.

Holly looked out the window. The sun was starting to come up. "You should get home to your kids."

"And you need to go get some rest too. Don't you dare open up shop until you've had a full night's sleep—well, morning's sleep. Come in at noon and file your story, if you think there's anything I said that can help."

"It'll be a human-interest piece," Holly said. "Your impressions of what happened in the last hour of Jordan's life."

Colette seemed dubious. "I wasn't all that focused on him."

"But he made that comment about you changing since high school. And you sat next to him at dinner. Did you two talk at all, before…?"

"I think he said something like, 'How delightful to be seated next to the guest of honor,' which I wasn't. I don't know if he was being sarcastic or what. My impression of him is that he wasn't such a nice guy."

"I won't say anything like that—since you're not sure, we'll keep to the facts. He was polite to you. Anything else? Did he look sick?"

"Not so I noticed." Colette thought about it. "Maybe he was sweating a little, but he'd been sitting by the fire, so I guess I thought it was probably hot right next to it. The fireplace is huge. And William kept adding more logs, so the thing was stoked."

Holly wrote those last bits down. She could work with that.

Chapter Five

On Saturday morning, over coffee, Bob read Holly's report about Jordan's death. Then he read it again. Apparently, she'd been an eye-witness right after the fact. God, how must she feel? He wanted to call her. She'd asked him about the condo development the other night. Maybe he could get some information together and send it to her—give her something else to think about and write about and plan for—or maybe he could ask her out to dinner and give her the materials himself. It was Saturday after all. And she was new in town. She wouldn't want to spend the weekend alone.

He closed his laptop, found her card in his wallet, and gave her a call before he could change his mind.

She answered on the first ring. "Bob!"

She had his number saved in her phonebook. And she sounded happy to hear from him.

"Hey, Holly, I just read your story about Jordan. I'm so sorry you had to see that, write about that, your first week in town."

"It's been a tough couple of days. First Ernie, now this."

"Yeah, I read about Ernie too. You are way better at keeping the online edition current than Ernie and Rachel were. We are lucky to have you."

"Thanks, Bob. It's a bit frantic. I've got all the *Trib* stuff to do, all those management-type details I know nothing about, plus my phone has been ringing off the hook. Everybody wants to know the inside scoop. Everyone has their own ideas about how Jordan died. Of course I have to tell people that the reports from the coroner and toxicology are not in yet. People keep asking me if the death was suspicious. I don't know what to say. The police told me not to speculate. They don't want me to report certain details. I don't know why. Just in case."

"I promise I wasn't calling to pump you for info." Bob wondered what Holly had held back from her news story.

"Oh, no, Bob, I know you weren't. I put a few numbers in my phonebook—people I wanted to hear from if they called—and you were one of them. I'm not answering any other calls today. I'm stressed out. My parents are frantic. You know Eddie and Courtney Fass are my aunt and uncle? They want me to come stay with them, in case people start knocking on the bungalow doors. I might do another update in a minute. Just 'condolences are pouring in'—something to help people feel they are being kept in the loop."

Bob let her vent. She needed a friend. He could be that person. "I was calling to ask you to dinner, but maybe you'll be with your aunt and uncle?" Was it too weird his therapist was Holly's aunt? Never mind. That wasn't important. Holly's stress level was the important thing right now.

"No, I just saw them on Thanksgiving. Was that only two days ago?"

"You could come here for dinner. I'm not right on the main road, like Blue Heaven is. It's very private here. I have a gate with a padlock on it, so nobody's going to bother you. And I broil a mean steak."

"Bob, that's so nice of you."

Before she could say no, he brought out his big guns, the thing he hoped to distract her with. "I have that information you wanted on the condo development. It might take your mind off Jordan, give you something else to focus on. Something else to write about. Give the town something else to talk about. This is kind of big news."

"Oh, Bob, that's perfect. It really is. What time should I come over? How do I get to your place?"

Bob gave Holly directions, hung up, and called his sister-in-law. Eva would know how to turn his bachelor pad into a place worthy of a date. Hell, she'd be ecstatic that he was finally moving on from Lily. Lily. Just thinking of her, just her name, evoked all those feelings he didn't like. So he switched off thoughts of Lily and focused on Holly. He liked thinking about Holly, and the ways she made him feel were mostly good. A little on edge, like he didn't want to fall into that love abyss again, but mostly good.

He tried looking at his place through Holly's eyes. Somehow, he didn't see a candlelit dinner being served on his island countertop. And he didn't have candles. Did they sell them in the grocery store?

After Eva agreed to fix up his place, a little too enthusiastically for Bob's comfort, he took the dogs to the groomer. He left them there for baths while he shopped for food. Home again, he realized he had forgotten candles. He could light the fire. That would be fine. He quickly printed off whatever he thought might help Holly spring this new condo and apartment development on the townsfolk. He had a price-range sheet from the developer, just estimates, but people would want to know. Holly had particularly asked about that. As he gathered everything into a large envelope, he realized he'd have to tell Daniel and Eva about the project before the news hit the papers. They might not be so happy. Eva owned Blue Heaven. It was the only resort in town, so the weekly rentals that were a part of the development plan would impact her business. And Daniel liked the fact that Blue Lake Woods was treed and undeveloped. Still, the developer had the zoning permits in place, and if it wasn't Bob drawing up the plans, someone else, someone from out of town, would. He marshaled his arguments and called his brother, hoping Eva would still get him a table and some dishes by six o'clock tonight.

****

Holly was in way over her head. Not only did she have the awful news of a death to cope with, but she had to do it alone. She'd worked all night on the story and this morning on the business end of things, which was so not her lane. It didn't help that the printer and the accountant and the advertisers all wanted to ask about Jordan's death. She was glad she had plans later. Maybe she'd fit in a nap, too. After all, she had a date. She needed her beauty sleep.

The phone rang. Holly glanced at caller ID. The police. "Yes?"

"Holly?"

"Yes? Sam? What is it?" She reached for pen and notebook.

Sam chuckled in a maddening way. "Chill, darlin'."

Darlin'? Not very professional! Also, where was he

from? Not downriver of Detroit, like her. That was a southern twang she heard. She tapped her pen against the notebook, waiting for him to fill her in. He took forever to ask her out.

"Sorry, could you repeat that?"

"I said, do you want to go out tonight?"

"What? Out? Like on a date?" Holly had to walk a fine line here. She couldn't just blow him off like she wanted to. He was a cop and an important source. She had to be professional even if he wasn't.

"Sure," Sam said, as if he hadn't given her a speeding ticket her third day in town. And made her late for her first assignment. Which had worked out okay, but still.

"I already have a date tonight, I'm sorry." She was really relieved to be telling the truth.

"Well, what about tomorrow? I might have some news for you."

She wanted to say *I can get the news off the police blotter, thank you very much*, but settled on "I'm so sorry, but I have to work. I'm running the paper on my own these days."

"Yeah, I heard about that. Well, maybe next weekend, then."

She made no comment but hung up thinking *no way in hell*.

Then she put in four hours of solid writing time before taking a shower and getting ready for dinner with Bob. No nap. On the way to his house, she stopped at the Farmer's Market. They had a great selection of greenery, and she picked out a little pine tree in a glazed pot for Bob. He could stick it on the porch, so the dogs wouldn't dig it up.

When Holly got to Bob's, she was glad she'd stopped by the drugstore and picked up a couple of chew toys, because the boys, as Bob called his dogs, clearly expected something of her. And when she pulled out the toys, they stopped trying to edge each other out of the petting contest and began nipping at the little stuffed furry things.

Bob admired the miniature pine tree and agreed it should stay on the porch. "Some Christmas plants are poisonous. Probably not trees. I have a pamphlet around here somewhere," he said. "And thank you. I'm not sure how the dogs will do with a full-sized tree. Even a fake one. So this is nice."

Holly thought it was sweet that he seemed a little nervous. She was too, but when she looked around his house, she felt immediately comfortable. You could tell so much about a person by the way they lived, the things they surrounded themselves with.

"Your house is amazing," she said, taking in the expanses of glass, the big room open to the kitchen, loft, and living area. A beautifully set little round table for two had been placed next to the crackling fire. Crystal wine glasses sparkled on the table.

"How are the dogs with the swags of green on the mantel?"

Bob had lit the pair of hurricane lamps that anchored the greens. A gorgeous bow on a pine wreath hung over the mantel picked up the gold tones on the edge of the pretty plates. Hanging under the mantel were two stockings for the boys, Corky and Sidney. They were of course red to match the tablecloth. Holly could not have created such a tableau herself. It was a work of art. "Bob, everything is so lovely."

"I didn't do it. Eva. My sister-in-law."

"Oh, well, good because I really don't like a man who is a better decorator than I am. But you designed this house, right?" Holly felt a warm glow that Bob would enlist someone to decorate for her. She hadn't given a thought to decking her own rented halls, but now she felt in the mood. "This place is a little jewel."

"Thank you. The condos will be more in this style. Lots of glass for views of wooded areas."

"Oh, the condos! I want one already."

"I'll take you to view the site tomorrow if you like."

"Yes, I would. Is it okay to get my photographer to take pictures to run with the article?"

"Sure. Hey, you want some wine?"

"I'd love a glass."

Bob pulled a bottle out of his fridge and opened it like a pro. "I noticed you drink Chardonnay, so I got a bottle of that and a red." He poured her a glass of the white. "Hope it's okay?"

Holly sipped. "It's great. You don't know how much I needed this night out. You are so sweet."

"Well, I hope you're hungry. I have sautéed mushrooms and baked potatoes. Eva loads them up with sour cream and cheese and bacon. The potatoes, I mean. I did the mushrooms myself." Bob stood over a pan, his wine glass in one hand, stirring the sizzling mushrooms. He turned down the heat like he was used to cooking on a stove, something Holly was not very good at. Not yet. But she could learn.

They sipped their wine while the steaks grilled out on the patio. Bob, like most men she knew—well, her dad and Uncle Eddie anyway—had a barbecue big as an oven on his patio.

While Bob flipped the steaks, Holly took a closer look at the picture on his mantel. It was Bob and a young woman. Lily Van Slyke. Holly's heart hammered. She'd forgotten about Lily and her ties to Bob for a minute. When Bob came back with the steaks, she brought the plates into the kitchen so he could dish out the food. Then they carried everything to the table in front of the fire and talked all through the yummy dinner about everything except Lily.

****

Holly's lush lips were stained with the red wine she'd switched to when he served the steak. Her blue eyes glowed in the light of the fire, setting off sparks of their own. The table Eva had found for him was small enough that he could reach over and kiss Holly if he wanted to. And he did. So he did. Her lips were warm, and her breath was sweet. He wished there wasn't a table between them.

Holly broke the kiss first, sitting back and smiling at him. "I like you," she said.

"And I like you, Holly."

"So Rachel set us up after all."

Bob laughed. He felt great. The food was good, the company was good, he had his dogs and a design project, which Daniel and Eva had reluctantly approved. All was right with his world. Then Corky barked, and Bob noticed both dogs standing at the front door. They'd behaved well during dinner, probably because Bob had bribed them with steak bones from the butcher. He let them out into the yard and stood watching, so they didn't wander far.

He'd kissed Holly. He supposed that meant he was

finally over Lily. He hadn't thought of Lily once tonight. Not all day in fact. The dogs quickly did their business in the frigid night air and came right back in, rushing up to Holly for pets, licking her fingers, sniffing at the table for treats.

"Boys! Go lie down." Bob had been training them all week, and they had caught on to the routine of lying on the oversized plaid pillows Eva and Daniel had bought for them. Of course, that was because they knew by now Bob would give them each a biscuit once they'd settled, which they quickly did.

He'd like to kiss Holly again. He went over to the table and tugged her hand. She let him lead her to the sofa. "I got dessert from the Two Sisters Bakery," Bob said. "Would you like it now or in a while?"

"You are spoiling me! Maybe in a minute. I do love that bakery. Those ladies are the ones who catered the Fun Divorce Club party."

"Yeah, they're great."

"I should have you over to my place for dinner and try them out." Holly's forehead crinkled.

"What?" Bob thought going to Holly's for dinner sounded great.

"I can't cook. Well, I do a mean pasta with sauce from a jar. And I make grilled cheese. But I want to have something special for you. And I don't want you to be my guinea pig as I learn to cook."

"Holly, it's fine if you don't cook. You write."

"I should do both. I've been living on Power Bars and Coke Zero."

Bob laughed. Holly was so much fun to be around. Not even death could get her down for long. But she hadn't known Jordan. Bob had. Maybe that was why he felt free of Lily. Jordan was dead, and he was alive. Had it taken death to make him feel alive again?

Bob put his arm around Holly, and she leaned into him with a sigh. He squeezed her shoulder, trying to comfort her. "Seeing Jordan, then having to write about him for the paper, had to be the worst."

"It was horrible." She nodded her head against his shoulder. "And people want to know cause of death. Of course. But for now I can only speculate, and I'm not willing to do that."

"Don't worry, Holly. Surely the police will have more information by Monday."

"Yes, I'm sure you're right. Tuesday at the latest, I'd think."

Bob reached out to smooth her bangs away from her face. Her skin was so soft. How did girls get such soft skin? But as he looked at Holly, her lashes covered her eyes, and he realized she was not a girl. She was a woman. He leaned in to kiss her again, and this time there was no table between them.

Soon, however, a cold nose inserted itself between them. Then another. Dog noses. Holly laughed and tugged at the paper Sidney held in his jaw.

"Give it to me, boy."

Sid released the paper. Bob noticed that Corky was playing in a pile of pamphlets that had fallen off his bookshelf. "What the…?" He got up and rescued the stack of information from the vet. "I need to file these things. Can you take a look? Is that page from the vet, too?"

"Yes." Holly scanned the paper. "It's the pamphlet about poisonous Christmas plants. Hey, I didn't know mistletoe was harmful."

"We didn't need mistletoe," Bob said, after she handed him the leaflet. He held on to her fingers for a minute and looked directly into her eyes, not breaking his gaze. She looked right back at him. Open. Trusting. It felt so good. Lily had never looked at him the way Holly did. He shoved the whole batch of vet papers onto a high shelf, then he kissed her one last time before she said she had to go.

Chapter Six

Holly woke later than usual. Still morning, barely. She brewed coffee and made a list. Order dinner from Two Sisters Bakery. Post quick request for memories of Jordan in the online edition. Write up Blue Lake Woods development project. Pick up dinner. Wash hair. A full day, right there.

The phone rang. Eva, her landlady, just wanted to alert Holly that a choir would be caroling in the gazebo on the property later. "Not a problem," Holly said. Hey, if people wanted to freeze to death while singing, who was she to stop them?

****

Bob went into town for a present for Holly. After her perfect gift of a real Christmas tree, he needed something special. At the hardware store, he tore himself away from the usual aisles and looked at all kinds of crap—well, not crap, but stuff women liked— teapots and kitchen towels with kittens on them. Nothing would do. Although he picked up a bottle at the wine shop to take to Holly, wine was just too ordinary. Finally, he went into a new store—well, new to him anyway—called Every Day Christmas.

"What are these angels supposed to do?" he asked the sales clerk.

"They're tree toppers."

"Oh." Bob thought about that. "You mean, they go

on the top of the tree? Like a Christmas tree?" Daniel had always put a star atop their tree, but maybe their mom would have liked an angel.

"Yes."

"I'll take that one." Bob pointed to the only angel that had dark hair like Holly's. "Gift wrapped, please."

Bob thought about getting flowers and candy but figured it would be overkill. He'd buy her flowers and candy for Valentine's Day.

****

Bob drove Holly out to see the site in Blue Lake Woods. There was nothing there at all but trees. Not yet, but she could imagine her new home nestled in among them. Bob said they'd have views of the Sapphire River in back. Holly was determined to have a river-view condo. This was her home.

The most thrilling part of the drive was being in the front seat with Bob. It was somehow so intimate. How had she ever thought he was dull when just sitting next to him made her shiver with excitement?

When they got back to the bungalow, Bob gave her a beautifully wrapped gift. And a bottle of wine. Holly lit the fire. No table in front of it, but they could sit there and drink hot chocolate spiked with Godiva liqueur.

"Unless you want a beer?" Holly offered. She'd bought some beer especially for Bob. And cheese, as she'd decided to order soup and a yummy sourdough from Two Sisters. Apple walnut pie for dessert, too. But she'd make her own grilled cheese sandwiches.

When her mom had asked Holly for ideas for Christmas gifts, she asked for a cookbook. The newfound domesticity worried Holly slightly. But she shook it off, reasoning that if she wanted her own home, she should know how to cook herself a proper meal. None of it had anything to do with Bob. Although he was nice. She really liked him now that she'd got to know him. He seemed totally over his heartbreak—well, except for the picture he still kept on his mantel. So she'd go slow. That was fine. She was too busy these days to invest much in a relationship. She wasn't sure what tomorrow would bring.

Bob came up behind her as she stood at the fridge lost in thought. He put one arm around her waist and reached the other inside the fridge for his beer. Holly decided to have a chocolate martini instead of hot chocolate. Dessert before dinner, but hey, it was the holidays. But first, she turned in Bob's arms, shut the fridge, and kissed him.

After dinner, they walked out to the registration room.

"There should be a flashlight in that drawer behind the registration counter," Bob said. Holly went to the drawer he pointed at and found the flashlight, which she handed to Bob. He opened a cleverly disguised door to the basement under the steps leading up to the second story. "I remember when we made this," he said.

"I didn't know you built this place!"

"Just the party room upstairs. It was my brother's project really. With Eva."

"Wow. Look at all this stuff."

The flashlight shone on box after box of decorations.

"It's not all for Christmas. There are beach toys, I think, too."

"Eva's so organized. Every box is labeled.

Impressive."

Bob had pulled out a half dozen boxes including the tree box.

"This has never been opened!" Holly checked out the pre-lit tree still sealed in the box. "Oh, that reminds me! Should I open your gift or keep it under the tree?"

"Open it after we get the tree up." Bob lifted the tree box like it was a file folder and carried it up the stairs. Holly stacked a few boxes of ornaments and followed him.

Holly had lit the fire up here earlier, so it would be toasty warm for Bob. The sky darkened outside, and it felt a little bit like being in a treehouse with all the big windows looking out over the pines in the yard. "Do you hear that?" Holly asked as Bob stuck the three pieces of the tree together and plugged in the lights.

"Oh, the choir."

"Yes." Holly went over to the window. The gazebo was lit from inside, wreathed in greenery and red bows, looking like something out of an enchanted dream. And the song rising up to her and Bob sounded heavenly. Made the mood magical. "Did Eva plan this for us?"

"Ha! I wouldn't put it past her, but no. They practice here a few times and then give a strolling concert downtown on Christmas Eve. They sort of walk the town to church for midnight mass."

"Christmas Eve is my birthday. 11:45 p.m." Holly felt shy for some reason. She busied herself pulling ornaments out of their box and hanging them on the tree.

Bob didn't say anything for a beat. Sweet voices floated up from the gazebo, surrounding them with song. At the end of the song, Bob said, "So that's why your name is Holly!"

And she blushed. Bob opened a box, unearthing a ball of mistletoe. He smiled and held it over her head, kissing her. They decided to take a short break from decorating the tree and moved over to the sofa, lips still touching.

****

Holly knew Monday would be difficult, but until she landed in it, she hadn't known to what degree it would fray her nerves. She only wanted to write, but she had to edit the outpouring of letters of remembrance from Jordan's friends and get that on the website. She knew a daily update, no matter how small and insignificant, was important. Today's article was a puff piece about holiday hours for local businesses, but it reminded her that she needed to speak to the accountant about advertising rates and lock in the December ads. While on the phone with him, she brought up the fact that she hadn't received a paycheck yet.

"You need to open a bank account and fill out the paperwork for direct deposit."

Funny, nobody had told her that. Really, did they think she was working for free? Then she felt ashamed. Poor Ernie, and Rachel was only helping her friend. The minute she hung up the phone, it started ringing and didn't stop for more than an hour as people called, wondering if the coroner's report was ready, and if so, what it said. Finally, Holly called the police station, but Amanda didn't know anything and Sam stonewalled her. Harlan, the chief, was not at the station, and no, Sam didn't know when he'd return. Holly wondered if she could call the county morgue directly, but then the phone rang again. This time it was her personal phone.

Tyler wanted to know why she would need pictures of trees. Holly wondered why he was not in school.

"Work study," he said.

"Okay then, work on taking a few pictures. I need that property specifically for a story." Thank the stars she'd written the piece about Bob's project yesterday and was putting it online today and in the print edition later. Tyler's photos always went in the print edition. "You're on deadline, remember," she told Tyler.

"Are you my new boss?" Tyler said.

"Yes." Holly hung up and then blew out a big breath when her phone and the office phone rang at the same time. She checked her own phone. The agent. Her heart skidded. She had to take this. At the rate her life was going, she may get an advance on a book she hadn't written yet before she saw a paycheck from the newspaper.

"Holly. How are those chapters coming?"

"In process." Well, it was true. She was processing the decision on whether she wanted to alienate her family or take a shot at making a decent living.

"When will you be done?"

"Soon. Very soon." She pulled a notebook and pen closer and wrote PRO and CON across the top of the page. "They're practically writing themselves."

"On that basis, I'm sending you a contract today. Sign it and return with the proposal within a week."

Holly thought that was getting very close to Christmas for the agent to be assigning deadlines. But the agent hung up before Holly could say anything. Well. She didn't know what to think. She'd have to make a complete list of pros and cons, read through the contract, find a lawyer to go over it, get Lily's permission, and her phone number...ugh, she didn't want to think about everything she had to do. One thing at a time, she told herself. She wanted a condo, and she needed to build her career. There were two things for the PRO list. This was an excellent opening. She had to walk through it. She wrote "fab opportunity" on the PRO list, then right away thought of three CONs. Eddie, Courtney, and Ruby. Damn. She called Colette, letting the office phone ring and ring.

"Hey, remember when you said you could give me a hand here?"

Colette said she felt good about helping out her mom and Holly. She told Holly she'd been back in Blue Lake a little over a month, and while she was still living with her mother, she needed to move forward. "A job is just the thing," she told Holly. "My kids are in school, and I don't have anything else to do. Also, I can't rely on my mom's charity forever. This way I'll earn my keep."

Colette arrived at an office in complete chaos. Holly was ready to have a meltdown, but she pulled herself together when Colette came through the door with two coffees from Perk next door. Holly was very grateful they wouldn't be drinking from the very old office pot.

"Oh, thank the stars you're here! I need to open a direct deposit, so I can start getting a pay check. Here, I made a list of what to do today. Tell me if it's okay."

Colette checked the list. She said she'd answer phones while Holly wrote copy. She could edit letters too. She could deal with the advertising budget. "Not a problem. Go on and set up your bank account. You need to get paid."

"Thanks." Holly had gotten the sleep Colette insisted she'd needed, but having Colette come in like this was the extra boost she needed. The insistent ring of the phone had been making her crazy. It was a lucky thing Colette had arrived when she did.

"Is it always like this?" Colette wanted to know.

"No. But then it's not every day someone is murdered in this town. I looked it up, and in fact, if it does turn out to be murder, this will be the first time. Ever. The last death in Blue Lake was justified homicide."

"Murdered? What do you know that I don't?" Colette asked.

"Nothing. Just speculation, based on what the whole town keeps saying when they call. Everyone's saying he was poisoned. The Two Sisters are out of their minds with worry that this will hurt their business, even though most of the Fun Divorce Club have sworn he didn't eat a bite." The phone rang again as if to punctuate Holly's statement.

"I say we switch the phone off for now. I'll make a recording telling people to read the latest in the online edition," Colette said. Holly could have kissed her. She'd never get a story written if she had to keep answering phones.

****

With Colette's expertise, the office was in good shape by midweek. Holly saw her first check land in her bank account. People seemed to love the Bob Bryman project, and the phone calls about Jordan slowed. Folks were shopping for Christmas. They seemed to expect the wheels of justice to grind slow.

Holly told Colette about the information in the

pamphlet from Bob's vet. And Colette remembered that there was a large ball of mistletoe above the piano bar in William's living room.

"Poisoning is a woman's murder weapon of choice."

"William did it," Colette said. "None of the women has the slightest motive."

"Not that we know."

"William is the guy. He was jealous because Jordan was dating his ex. That's motive. And William had the means, too. His mistletoe. And opportunity—his house."

"Well, yes, but we have to see what happens with the coroner."

Thursday, the coroner released the report. Death by poisoning. The police called William "a person of interest."

Now that Colette had taken care of the editorial and office management, Holly found time to bang out three rough chapters and an outline. On Friday, the agent called, reminding Holly of her deadline. Holly needed to sign the contract and get it back to her by Monday.

Holly had found the perfect PRO that trumped all CONs. Her parents would not have to worry about her; their investment in her college education would not go to waste if she signed the contract and was able to support herself after her very short lease on Blue Heaven ran out.

Now all she needed was a lawyer. And Lily's phone number. For that, she needed Bob.

****

Holly's peppermint latte cooled as she sat in Perk across from Bob wondering exactly how to bring up the subject of Lily. It didn't help that Bob was currently describing the next wonderful date he'd planned for them. A sleigh ride.

"Are you still in love with Lily?"

Bob's eyes widened. He blinked. "Ah…"

"No, listen, sorry, it's not my business."

"It's okay." Bob zipped his coat up and down a few times. "I'm not. I was for a long time. Then I got the dogs, and something in me switched gears."

Dogs? Really?

"I've been seeing someone—"

"Someone else?!" Holly couldn't keep up with this guy.

"No, not that. Not like you. A shrink. She thinks I was caught in a pattern or something. I don't know. She told me to get the dogs, and sure enough it worked."

"That's good." Holly wondered if he'd be okay with the book. So far she didn't get a good vibe from people about it.

"Yeah. Lily's in Detroit now. She's a P.I." Zip. Zip. "She changed her name."

"Why?"

"I don't know. She won't talk to me. She said we both need to move on. I just wish I had listened to her sooner."

"What's her new name? No, wait, don't tell me."

"Why not?"

"I have to tell you…I was interested in Lily's story before I ever came to Blue Lake. As a writer."

Bob seemed confused.

"It just…you know my family connection." She set down her coffee and wiped her sweaty palms on her jeans. "I read every scrap I could about Lily and the way she stood up for herself despite everything going against her." Holly thought about the way Lily had saved Ruby. How she had shot Ruby's rapist. Killed him. And then how she had gone on to trap her own father in a sting operation so that he admitted to Lily he had killed her mother, something Lily had long suspected. Then Lily's father had tried to cover up that crime by murdering the mechanic who had tampered with Lily's mother's car. It was all about money. Lily's mother's money, held in trust for Lily. After her dad went to jail, Lily had disappeared. Now Holly had the final piece of the puzzle. But she'd obtained it in a way that made her feel sleazy.

"What is it, Holly?"

"Okay. Well, you know I need to make a living. So, the reporting pays basic bills. Eva is not charging me much rent. So I'm good for now, but what about after tourist season starts? I want to buy a condo, but I need a better income. My original idea was to write true-crime books as well as report news. That would supplement my income, if I could do it."

Light dawned in Bob's eyes. Holly didn't like the subtle distrust that began to settle over his features.

"Oh, I know what you're thinking, but Bob, it was before I met you."

"You were going to tell Lily's story. That's why you were so interested in me." Bob abruptly stood.

"No, honestly." She grabbed his hand before he could leave. "Sit down. Listen to me. This is hard."

Bob reluctantly sat back down. "I'm only doing this because I really like you Holly. Or I did like you."

"It's true. I did have the idea to write about Lily. I brought it up to my uncle Eddie, and he said I could not write about Ruby. I could not mention her name or our family connection. Aunt Courtney said Lily wouldn't be happy, either. So I said I'd ask to interview her for the book, and if she said no, I wouldn't write it."

Bob looked at first disgusted, then relieved. Holly tried to read him, but it was difficult. Since they'd begun this intense conversation, the noise level had gone way up. That was good, but all the people milling around ordering scones and coffees and croissants was not good. Was that Sam at the counter ordering a donut? Damn.

"Really?" Bob finally said. "You would just give up the idea? Because it's a good one. I mean, I'm not saying write the book, but I can see how it would be something that might get you a publisher." Bob was not meeting her eyes, which had Holly a little worried.

"Bob, if I don't write that book, somebody else will. I have an agent interested, and she'll shop the idea if I give it up. But I need Lily's phone number. Before I decide anything, I need to talk to her."

"I don't have her number. And I'm not sure I'd give it to you if I did. I feel used, Holly."

"I knew you would. That's why I couldn't tell you. But I'm telling you now. That should count for something."

He nodded, but she could tell he remained unconvinced. "Just promise whatever you decide, you won't use anything I have told you in confidence."

"Well, you didn't tell me much. Not even her new name."

"Yeah, I don't think I will. I feel protective of her. You don't understand, Holly. She's not like you. She's fragile."

69

Holly doubted that. Fragile? Working in Detroit? As a P.I.? That didn't add up. But she knew not to push Bob.

"The only way to write the book so I don't upset a bunch of people is to interview Lily herself."

"She'd never agree to that. She doesn't even want to talk to me, and I'm not trying to use her to further my own career."

Ouch. That hurt. But it was true, if only in the way the subject of every single story she wrote was being used. Didn't everyone use each other all the time? In a way? Wasn't that true? Not that she'd say so to Bob.

Bob got up again. "Are we through?"

Damn, that sounded like a break-up. They'd hardly gotten together. "Unless you want to talk more," she said.

"No, thanks." Bob walked out without looking back. Holly guessed that meant no sleigh ride.

Chapter Seven

"Trouble in Paradise?" Sam bit into his donut with gusto.

Holly threw her empty coffee cup away, not even bothering to reply. She walked back to the *Tribune*, but before she could even say a word to Colette about what had just happened with Bob, the bell over the door jingled. Sam. Holding two coffees.

"Sorry," Sam said to Colette, raising the coffees and his shoulders in a helpless man shrug.

"Not a problem," Colette said. "I'm just leaving for lunch. But first, any suspects in the murder?"

"No. And it's poisoning, period. Could be accidental." He didn't sound too convinced. "Why?" he asked Colette. "You gotta theory?"

"It was Will."

Holly let out a huge sigh. Colette had been going on and on about how Will killed Jordan, but Holly didn't buy it. Just because Colette thought he was an arrogant asshole. If every arrogant asshole in the world committed murder, there wouldn't be any nice people left.

Colette hitched her purse on her shoulder. "I'll just be next door," she said.

As soon as she left for Perk, Sam grabbed her chair and wheeled it over to Holly's desk. He plopped the coffee down. "Mocha latte. Thought you could use a hit of chocolate after that public harsh."

"Thanks," she said.

"So what's the deal with you and Bryman? I thought he was hung up on Lily Van Slyke."

"We're just friends. Or we were." What the hell. She might as well talk to him. He didn't seem to be going anywhere.

"That's not what I heard."

Amanda. When Holly called for the police blotter updates, she usually told Amanda what she was doing that evening. And last weekend had been All About Bob. Sigh.

"So let's go out," Sam said.

"I've got too much work."

"What? Here? You're kidding, right?"

"No. And I'm writing a book, too."

"Like as a hobby?"

"No again. It's a real job. I have a contract." So what if it remained unsigned? Which reminded her of that other item on her list: she still didn't know Lily's last name, still didn't have her phone number.

"Oh. What's your book about?"

"Lily Van Slyke."

"Huh. So that's why you were seeing Bryman. He give you anything useful?"

"Not really."

"What do you need?"

"Did you know she changed her name?"

"Yeah. I have lots of information on her. Maybe you should have tried dating me first."

If Holly wasn't an adult, she'd stick out her tongue. She bit it instead. "I might go out with you if you have a name and phone number."

"I can get you that information."

What a reporter wouldn't do for a story.

****

Friday night, Holly went to a movie with Sam. It was an action flick, naturally. She was only putting up with him because he had something she wanted. Had she done the same thing with Bob? No. She'd really liked Bob. Sam was arrogant. He had some kind of macho mask on or something. She couldn't feel the real Sam under his bravado. It was a turnoff. So was the film. And so was the dark bar he'd taken her to for wings and beer afterward. Wasn't she worth at least a nice restaurant?

She dunked a wing in blue cheese sauce and chewed it, thinking about the story she needed to write when she got home. Sam was talking about the movie and how the sections that involved police work had been totally unrealistic.

After five minutes of elaborately boring cop talk, Holly let most of what Sam said float away. She listened for inflection so she'd know if he asked her a question, which seemed unlikely. When he finally stopped his in-depth analysis of a third-rate film, she said, "What is that accent, anyway?" She didn't want to be rude and say she thought the whole picture was unrealistic so therefore a waste of time to discuss, but she had to say something. "Where are you from, Sam Carpenter? And was your father a carpenter?"

Sam snorted, obviously pleased she was paying attention to him. He thought she was interested, and maybe she was. A little bit. But it was really the reporter in her. She was naturally curious about people. And he was not hard on the eyes. Not at all. She'd been on worse dates. Many worse dates. Of course, nobody had bribed her for a date before, but that was a little bit flattering. Sam might be the best-looking guy she'd ever gone out with. He must be used to prom queens.

"Cincinnati. Came here for the job. And my dad is a plumber not a carpenter. What does your dad do?"

"He's in IT."

"For the autos?"

"Of course."

"My mom works too. She's a sales rep. She works massive hours. My dad kind of raised us more than she did. I have a sister and a brother. You?"

"My mom didn't work when I was growing up, but she does garden design now."

Holly couldn't believe they were having an actual conversation. She had figured he didn't talk much, since he'd taken her to a film on their first date. Not that she was thinking there would ever be another one. But she had to admit it was nice to do something besides work this weekend. Sure, a sleigh ride would have been better, but here was a guy actually interested in her.

"You have brothers and sisters?"

"Just me. That's interesting about your dad."

"Yeah. I used to go on jobs with him and hand him his tools. We saw a lot of ugly toilets."

"Did your mom cook dinner?"

"My dad picked up dinner from restaurants most nights. She didn't eat with us much."

That explained why he was not so good with charming. He didn't really know how to deal with females. It was kind of sad. Also sad, Bob hadn't texted, not even once since he'd left her in Perk earlier in the week, even though she'd texted him twice. Just about random stuff. "Snow!" was one. Lame.

"So what's Lily's last name?"

"White. You want another beer?"

"I'm good. I have to go home and write a story."

"Really? You weren't just trying to get out of the date?"

"Nope, really."

"Because I have her address too."

She pulled her pad out of her purse. "Phone number?"

He nodded. "This is all off the record. I'm like, a confidential source, okay?"

"Of course. I don't reveal my sources."

"Sometimes they reveal themselves for you."

He meant Amanda. She laughed but didn't comment. She was too busy scribbling down all the things he told her about Lily White, which was a weird choice for a new name. So ordinary. If Holly could pick her own name she'd go with something French.

Holly felt so grateful for the help with the book that when Sam asked for another date, she said maybe the following weekend. For now, she really did have to work on the book. And she had to call Lily, too.

****

Saturday morning, Holly called Lily right after coffee and a shower. She was stunned, when, after so long thinking about her, Lily answered her phone on the first ring. Lily listened to Holly's pitch, then said, no, she did not authorize anybody to write anything about her life.

"Why can't you people just leave me alone?" Lily blurted before hanging up the phone. Holly didn't call back. Apparently, she wasn't the only one with the brilliant idea to get Lily to talk on the record. Even if it was a story showing that Lily was an innocent victim. Maybe Lily didn't want to be a victim. Holly supposed that was admirable, but what did it mean for her and her own aspirations?

Was her idea of becoming a true-crime author silly? Wishful thinking? Would a career built on this story truly mean not caring about who she hurt in service to the story? Would every book thereafter mean invading innocent people's closely guarded privacy and intruding on whatever carefully rebuilt life they were trying to live after evil had wrecked their lives? Why did she ever think Lily would be okay with that? Well, she hadn't thought about Lily's approval or disapproval at all. Not until people had forced her to look at it.

Holly was suddenly very glad it was the weekend and she had little more to do than stare at the yawning chasm that was her future. She didn't think she could write a news story to save her life right now. After two weeks of nonstop writing, she felt paralyzed with a kind of shocked sadness. She was disappointed in herself. She was sad. She was lonely. She was a failure.

Okay, stop it, she told herself. You are not a failure. You single-handedly wrote every article for the paper until Colette came on board. That is not nothing.

The phone rang. Colette. She must have ESP.

"Hey, Colette. What's up?"

"Can you get down here to the paper?"

There went Holly's day off. No time for burnout in this business. "I'll be there in ten," Holly said.

At the *Trib*, Colette dropped the bombshell. "Will was arrested. I knew it. Sam must have taken my suspicions seriously."

"Do you suppose this means there's no chance the poisoning was accidental?"

"Looks like, but no confirmation on that."

Holly started typing a quick report stating that Will had been arrested but giving no details, because she had none. She typed with one hand and called Sam with the other.

Amanda answered. "Sam booked him. He's being photographed and fingerprinted now."

"Thanks, Amanda," Holly said. "Any idea about the exact cause of death? Like what poison was administered? And how? And when?"

"I'm not supposed to say."

"Okay, but off the record?"

"I can't say, hon."

"Do they know the poison?"

Colette's eyebrows shot to her hairline.

"Yes, but they don't want that information released yet. Shit. Don't write that. Nobody is supposed to know. It's not official."

"Okay." Holly stopped typing. She tried again. "Was it a holiday plant?"

"How did you know?"

"Lucky guess."

"Yeah, well, please don't print it. I have to go."

"Okay, but what about motive?"

"Why do you want to know if you're not printing this?"

"Curious."

Amanda sighed. Her love of gossip clearly warred with her need for discretion. "Sam says he smells evil, but that's not true. Now I really have to go."

Before Holly had even put down her phone, Colette was off on a tangent. "I bet he had means. That's the evidence for arrest. Think about it. It was his house. He could have poisoned Jordan's food or beverage and left everyone else's alone. He made it a point to pour my first drink. He must have done that for everyone. What's his motive?"

"Sam said he smells evil. Amanda disagrees."

Holly didn't say that was unprofessional of Sam. She'd never even met Will, but she tended to agree with Amanda.

Holly stared at her screen, feeling Colette's eyeballs on her the entire time. She typed another sentence. "Okay, it's ready. Without all the conjecture." She sent it over to Colette to edit and post online. Colette did so quickly. People would start phoning any minute.

Holly went over to Perk for two coffees. When she got back, Colette was already on the phone. She hung up after saying, "No comment," then she put a recording on the phone saying they were working on a story and had no further information about Will's arrest but that the online version would be updated as soon as they had any new information.

"They can call the police if they want more info," Colette said. Holly knew this is why Colette was the manager and she was the writer. She'd never have thought of that.

"So Amanda said it was a Christmas plant. I'm thinking mistletoe."

"The mistletoe murder!"

"Yeah. But it slipped out. Amanda says they want to keep it away from the public for now. If it gets out, it could impede their investigation."

"Probably still looking for evidence and don't want citizens tampering with Will's garbage and stuff."

"Was there mistletoe in the house?"

"Yep. A big wad of it over the piano bar."

"Okay, well, certain kinds of mistletoe can be deadly for humans."

"Who says?"

Holly told Colette about the pamphlet at Bob's house. Then she sighed. Bob still hadn't texted her. Even after she'd texted that she'd spoken to Lily. She thought for sure he'd want to know about that. Not that she knew what she was going to do. For now, her plan was to tell the agent she'd spoken to Lily briefly but needed to follow up, maybe after the holidays. Holly clicked her mind over to the other matter at hand.

"Did Will smell evil to you?"

Colette looked pensive. "Not really. Only evil in the way conceited men can be, you know, like they understand you want them and so does everybody else. But I'm not a cop. They have a sixth sense."

Holly wasn't sure about Sam's sixth sense. "It's a crappy motive. Smelling evil. I don't think it even would count in a court of law."

"Probably not," Colette agreed. "They need the mistletoe, and the tox screen needs to prove it was the same mistletoe—I don't know—from the same tree or whatever."

"They were selling mistletoe at the Farmer's Market last week."

"Yeah. They have it every year."

"So anybody in town could have got some."

"I just don't think this is enough to hold him for

long. I bet he has a lawyer." Colette's cell phone rang. "It's my mom," she said.

Holly checked her texts. Still nothing from Bob. She was giving herself the weekend to decide what to do about the Lily book. Unauthorized, or forget the whole thing. Those were her choices.

Meanwhile, she decided to get a list of everyone who was at the Fun Divorce Club the night of the murder. If Will's attorney got him out of jail, Holly wanted to have background on every other person who could possibly have poisoned Jordan. It had to be someone in the house that night. The caterers or a member of the Fun Divorce Club. Holly didn't think it was the caterers. Their motive was nonexistent. Their careers depended on NOT poisoning people. And the poison was not food, but a Christmas plant. A poisonous Christmas plant. She couldn't print it, but she added it to her top secret notebook, which she'd started bringing to work to record all the suppositions and theories about the Fun Divorce Club murder. When, she wondered, had she stopped writing about Lily in her notebook and started tracking a current murder mystery? Because, for sure, it was murder.

When Colette hung up the phone, Holly was ready with recorder, pen, and notebook. "Tell me everything you know about every single person at the party that night."

"Mom says good job."

"How's Ernie?" Holly felt bad she hadn't asked first thing.

"Pretty good. He says thanks for the flowers."

Holly waited a beat, then when Colette didn't say anything else about Ernie, plunged ahead. "Okay, so if it's not Will, if he is not the murderer, which you have to admit is possible, then I want to know as much as possible about other suspects. So, names. And possible motive." Everyone at that party had the means and the opportunity. It remained to be seen who had a motive.

"I don't know. Maybe they have more evidence than you think. I mean, really, I can give you those names, but you're making this too difficult. It was Will."

Colette gave her the names, but Holly couldn't help thinking about what further evidence the cops had. Later, at home, she called Sam.

"Off the record?"

"Sure," Holly said.

"What about another date?"

Jeez. What kind of a cop used extortion to get a date?

Holly said she was too busy with work and hung up.

She'd missed three calls from the agent. Finally, she texted her a flimsy excuse that had a very slight relationship with the truth.

If only Bob would text her, that might give her some incentive to stop the book. Wait. Why did it matter to her so much what Bob thought? In his own inflated opinion, he was ethically far above her. Who needed a guy like that?

Chapter Eight

Bob sat across from Dr. Fass explaining why he felt ethically Holly was in the wrong to write about Lily.

"But you just said Holly texted you and said she wasn't going to write about Lily."

"Well, she kind of said that. See, first she said she wouldn't write about Lily unless Lily agreed. So Lily did not agree. But that doesn't mean Holly won't change her mind and write an unauthorized book. She wants to buy a condo."

Dr. Fass looked concerned. Belatedly, Bob remembered Holly was her niece. "Oh, sorry. I know you're related."

"It's fine."

"But how are you handling it? I mean, don't you feel angry? Because I do."

"What exactly are you angry about?"

Bob noticed that Dr. Fass didn't answer his question. That's fine. He knew there were lines you didn't cross in therapy. But it was frustrating. He didn't need a therapist right now, he needed a friend.

"Can I fire you?"

Dr. Fass rephrased. She was very good at rephrasing. "You'd like to end therapy?"

"Yes. Not because you didn't help me. You did. But I think I'm over Lily. I'm worried about her, yes.

But I haven't been focused on her much at all lately. I have the dogs, and I have my new design project. I'm keeping busy. This thing with Holly just seems like a normal dating problem."

"It does. And you are doing well, Bob. I'm pleased you see that. I think we can agree to end therapy with the understanding that you can call me any time you feel you need someone to talk to."

"Okay, well, can we talk as friends now?"

"Not if you want to talk to me about my niece. I will say, I think you're right, what you and Holly have is a normal dating problem. The way Eddie and I are handling this situation is to trust Holly. She's family. We give her the benefit of the doubt. You have to decide for yourself if you are willing to do that."

"No, yeah, you're right. You've been great. Really. Thank you." Bob left Dr. Fass's office feeling lighter and heavier at the same time. Mental health sort of sucked.

****

Holly recognized the woman with the big pile of stuff at the Farmer's Market. India. Jordan's ex. Will's ex. Everybody in the Fun Divorce Club's ex. Holly had yet to learn to cook, and she wasn't even buying vegetables or fruit to eat raw. She was at the Farmer's Market to buy mistletoe and maybe find out when Will had purchased his.

"Don't you have anything?" India said, indicating that Holly could go ahead of her.

"No, it's fine. I was looking for mistletoe. Looks like you bought it up." The cashier was ringing up India's purchases when India plucked a bunch of mistletoe from her pile.

"For you," India said. Then, "Hey, aren't you the new reporter for the *Tribune*?"

Holly smiled. "Yes, Holly. And you're India."

"How'd you know?"

"Reporters know stuff."

India laughed.

"Why all the holiday greenery? You must have a really big house."

"Oh, so something you don't know! I'm an interior decorator. I'm doing a bunch of houses for the holidays."

Holly had never heard of hiring out your Christmas decorating, but that didn't mean it never happened. Had Will hired out his decorating to India? If so, that would mean India had purchased the mistletoe, not Will.

"That's so wonderful. Would you consider me doing a profile on you? I'm looking for good holiday stories. Maybe you could give readers a few tips for quick festive touches? And of course we'll mention your business, maybe get you some jobs?" Holly thought interviewing India would be easier than just bombarding her with questions. Plus, she really thought it would be a good story.

"Sure," India said. They made a date for lunch at Perk. Holly paid for her sprig of mistletoe and left.

The agent was relentless. Holly had stopped picking up her phone. She knew if she didn't do something fast, she would lose the contract. She tried to focus on her interview with India, and gathering facts and rumors from Colette and Amanda and the Internet. India had gotten her second divorce because of Will, or so Amanda said. "They say she was pregnant, but she never did have a third baby, so that may just be a rumor." Holly was pretty sure the divorce thing was a rumor too but an intriguing one.

Passion could be crazy. Had Jordan broken up with India? Had Will? Was she a woman scorned enough to kill? To plot a sick revenge like murdering one ex-lover and then pinning the blame on another?

****

India met Holly at Perk as planned. She asked Holly if she wanted to split a turkey club panini.

"Oh, that's my favorite," Holly said. Damn. She was starting to like India.

They talked about India's education and experience. Holly got three cute holiday décor ideas even she could use, like swapping out a poinsettia plant instead of the usual centerpiece—"Especially if your centerpiece consists of salt and pepper shakers plus a butter dish"—on the kitchen table.

"Unless you have a cat," said India.

"Poisonous?" Holly ventured.

"Yep." The mention of poison did not faze India. Either she was a very cold-blooded killer, or she didn't do it. Holly made a show of putting her recorder away. She thanked India for the interview.

"No, thank you," India said. "You're giving my business a boost, and I appreciate it."

"Decorated many houses of the holidays yet?"

"Just Will's, because he had the party." A sad expression crossed India's features, but there was no guilt.

Holly added India to the "who-probably-did-not-do-it" column of her notebook. She needed to be more organized. Like, everyone should have their own page, each person in the Fun Divorce Club. And each of them should have two columns, "Why they may have done it" and "Why they probably didn't do it." Whoever had the most reasons in the first column would be the most likely suspect. But she couldn't do it now, because India was sitting there looking at her. She stashed her notebook and fished for a new topic.

"Can't be easy being a single mom," Holly said. When India looked startled by the change in tone to something more personal, Holly added, "We're off the record now."

"Oh. Well, yeah. It's not easy. The Fun Divorce Club helps. Helped."

"Yeah, it's too bad about Jordan." Holly noticed a flicker of something skitter across India's face. Distaste, she thought. "What?" Holly hoped India would say something about her feelings for Jordan.

"Well. Not to speak ill of the dead, but Jordan was a sleaze." India used such a low tone of voice Holly could hardly hear her. But she was pretty sure India had said "sleaze" not "squeeze."

Holly scooted her chair closer to India. "How so?"

India looked uncomfortable.

"I'm not going to write a *Trib* column about it," Holly said, her voice low to match India's. "I promise I won't even mention it at all."

India squirmed in her seat.

"Never mind," Holly said, feeling bad for her. She really didn't think India could murder Jordan and frame Will for it. She didn't have that kind of super-smart psychopath vibe. "Don't say anything you'd rather not."

"It's not that…well, Ruby Fass is your cousin, right?"

Why Ruby's name had come up, Holly had no idea, but she nodded her head. "Sure, she's my little cousin. Do you know Ruby?"

"Well, my daughter is friends with her. They're fifteen, right?"

"Yeah, that sounds right." Holly had no idea what two fifteen-year-old girls had to do with Jordan's death. They were certainly not old enough to be in the Fun Divorce Club. She was quiet for a few beats, letting the silence fill the space between them at the table.

"So, Jordan," India finally said, "was sort of hitting on my daughter. While we were dating."

Wow. That might be a motive for murder. Holly didn't have direct experience with being a mom, but the look in India's eye spelled fierce love and something else. That was a total mom thing. Look at the way Aunt Courtney had been so protective of Ruby at Thanksgiving. Heck, even her own mom was like a lioness when it came to protecting Holly. India was right; Jordan was a sleaze. But that didn't mean India killed him. Or did it?

"Like, how did he hit on her?" Holly remembered Ruby's near-rape experience a few summers ago and shuddered.

"Nothing like what happened to Ruby," India said, correctly reading Holly's shudder. "He just would...I don't know."

Now India was into her story. She leaned all the way over the table, arms crossed, hands holding opposite elbows as if that would help her to keep calm. But her eyes said she was still anything but calm when it came to her teenage daughter. "At first, I thought he was just getting to know my kids, you know, being nice to them. But after a while, I noticed he was really just focusing on Whitney and ignoring the two younger kids." She took a breath and looked around. "I noticed Whitney was acting nervous around him. She would stick her tongue out or roll her eyes if I said he was coming over. I called her on it one day, you know, in a nice way. I said, 'Honey, is there a reason you don't like Jordan? Is he bothering you?' You know, saying all the things they tell you to say when you want to know if your child is being interfered with." India had been staring intensely into Holly's eyes, but now she lowered her lids, and a few tears, quickly brushed away, sneaked out.

Holly impulsively put her hands over India's wrists. "I'm sorry I asked. I had no idea. You don't have to say anything else."

"No." India looked up again. "I want to, I want to finish. It wasn't that bad. He hadn't touched her inappropriately or anything. But he had made comments that had her feeling uncomfortable. When I asked what he said, she said once he'd told her she was hot. And that added to the extra attention he always paid her just was too much."

"So you broke up with him?"

"Next time he came over, I ran outside, kicked his car door, and told him to never come back. I put a little dent in it. Hurt my foot, too. I almost quit the club after that, but Phoebe talked me into staying. She always had a soft spot for Jordan. More fool her. She said he'd made an error in judgment, that he had some idea he was giving Whitney confidence or something."

Holly patted India's shoulder. "It must be so hard being a single mom," she said again.

"It is. But it's better than being married and miserable. And I wouldn't trade my kids for anything."

"No, of course you wouldn't."

Just then another woman came in, towing a toddler.

"That's Phoebe," India said. "From the Fun Divorce Club. The one who stuck up for Jordan. She even dated him after I did."

Holly wrinkled her nose. "Eww."

"I know. But it's hard finding a guy when you're a single mom. Most guys our age just go for the younger ones who aren't married yet. Like you. Jordan would have eaten you with a spoon."

Phoebe ordered a coffee and a cookie for her toddler, then she and her cute little girl came up and said hi to India. India introduced Holly.

"Nice to meet you, Phoebe," Holly said. "And thanks for the Christmas story, India. I better get back to work and write it." Phoebe was already sitting down and making herself comfortable. Holly felt sorry for her. Why would anyone date a guy who hit on teenagers?

Holly shuddered, then bought a mocha latte to help her warm up, forget Jordan, and write up the puff piece on India.

"I'll get that," Bob said, thrusting money at the cashier for Holly's latte.

Holly, startled, almost dropped her coffee on his feet. "Bob, I didn't hear you come in."

"No. You were thinking pretty hard there. Big story?"

"Yes. Um, thanks for this." She lifted her paper cup and smiled. Bob looked happy. Chipper, even. Holly started to leave Perk. She had to write up her story on India. She had to ask Colette if she'd heard any rumors about Jordan's sexual proclivities.

"How's the true-crime career going?"

Holly stopped before she reached the door. Bob indicated their favorite table with his coffee cup. Hmm. India and Phoebe walked past them, out the door. India winked at her and waved on her way out. Holly took a seat. The puff piece could wait. "I wanted to speak to you about that."

"Sorry I didn't answer your texts. I've been busy with the new project. And I heard you were dating Sam now, so…"

"I had one date with Sam. We didn't click. But anyway, I spoke to Lily, and she didn't want me to write about her, so I haven't signed the contract."

Bob's face visibly relaxed. "So do you think Will is guilty?" He'd changed the subject before Holly could get into the details of her pro and con list. And the fact that the offer was still in her back pocket, should she choose to accept it and write an unauthorized story.

"I don't know." Holly was happy to answer his question about Will, happy to pursue a different topic. "I think everyone seems pretty quick to condemn him, but that makes me wonder if people just want somebody to blame so they can get back to their lives."

Bob nodded. "Especially during the holidays."

Holly went back to work slightly happy and slightly depressed. She and Bob were friends again, but he didn't seem to want to take her on a sleigh ride any time soon.

Chapter Nine

"Holly," Colette said. "I need the Fun Divorce Club."

Holly held the phone to her ear, trying to process Colette's words.

"Why?" she finally said.

Colette went on to tell her Jenny was sick with the flu, Leroy had a black eye, and Heather was not speaking to her. "Will you be okay today without me? I can edit and manage from home for today, but my little one is puking and has a fever. I'm taking her to the pediatrician in an hour."

"Oh. Poor Jenny. Sure, I'll hold down the fort."

"Thanks, Hols." Colette hung up the phone.

A few hours later, Colette called again. "Well, one problem solved," she told Holly. "Jenny has the flu. And a temp just a pinch above normal. Clear foods for a day and lots of rest. She should be fine in the morning. God willing."

"What's your other problem?"

"Oh, honey, I've got more than one. Take my daughter, Heather." Colette went on to describe how when Heather was small like Jenny, mom and daughter had been best friends, just the two of them against the world. Heather had worshipped Colette. Wanted nothing to do with her daddy, who wasn't home much anyway. "Now she wants to move back to Florida and live with Mitch."

"Oh gee. I'm so sorry, Colette. Anything I can do?"

"No, just keep writing. God willing, tomorrow morning Jenny will wake up and be just fine."

"So what was the other problem?"

"Leroy absolutely refuses to tell me where he'd gotten his black eye. Also Heather just texted me, from across the kitchen no less, that she needs her pink sweater for school tomorrow *if it wasn't too much trouble*."

"I guess you do need the Fun Divorce Club." Holly had no experience in being a mom or even an aunt. She'd done a little babysitting, but that had been years ago.

"You know, the *Tribune* is more than a job, it's a family legacy. My father took over the paper from my grandfather, who had inherited it from his father. Now it's my turn, since my brother works on oil rigs in the Pacific and has no desire at all to move home to Blue Lake and take over the family business. I have to step in, and I'm enjoying it. Except Heather seems to resent the fact that I have a job, despite never wanting to speak to me again. Oh, no, Jenny just threw up again. Gotta go."

Holly made a note to call and check on Colette later.

She definitely, certainly, one-hundred-percent needed the Fun Divorce Club.

India had a daughter in Heather's class, and Kelly had been through the teen years already. The guys would know what to do about Leroy's black eye. Of course with Jordan dead and Will in jail, that only left

Patrick and Quinn for the guy component of the group.

Colette came to work the next morning, so Holly hoped everything had somehow righted itself.

Colette sat down across from Holly and sighed.

Holly looked up from her laptop. "What?"

Colette explained her dilemma. She was hosting the Fun Divorce Club, but she couldn't do it at her mother's since she wanted to discuss her children and they'd be there.

"Hey, why don't you use Blue Heaven? It has that nice room upstairs I almost never use. Bob and I decorated it so cute for Christmas."

"Oh, that's so sweet, Holly. That might work. Maybe I can get my mom to leave Ernie's side to watch the kids for a night."

"What about Heather?" Holly asked.

"Still the same."

"No, I mean, when I was her age, I was babysitting already. Maybe she would treat you better if you gave her a little responsibility. And paid her ten bucks an hour."

"Huh. I never thought of that."

Colette took out her phone, apparently texting Heather.

****

Holly wondered how she could possibly get an invitation to the Fun Divorce Club meeting at Blue Heaven on Friday night. Maybe she could offer to make the food? But then, she still couldn't cook. She could buy chips and dip and cheese and crackers and vodka and wine. She imagined divorced people liked to drink at their meetings, where they...what? Complained about their kids? Flirted with each other? Plotted murder?

Holly was still not convinced Will murdered Jordan. For one thing, the supposed evidence contradicted itself. On the one hand, Colette claimed Will was an arrogant lady's man. In her next breath, she said Will was jealous of Phoebe and Jordan. He couldn't be both, could he? It didn't add up, not in Holly's mind anyway. So that meant someone else in the Fun Divorce Club was a murderer. And she had just given permission for that person to come to Blue Heaven. Damn!

****

Holly had no reason to join the Fun Divorce Club meeting. Colette had brought the snacks and drinks and insisted Holly didn't have to listen for the door. "I'm perfectly fine staying down here to greet the guests. You go ahead into your private area and work on your book."

Colette knew Holly was working on the proposal. Unlike Bob and her family, she didn't see anything wrong with it. In fact, Colette said she admired Holly's ability to snag the attention of a New York literary agent. "That just doesn't happen in Blue Lake," she had told Holly.

Instead of working on her book, though, Holly started researching mistletoe. She got so involved with her research, at first she didn't even hear the sounds of the meeting wrapping up a few hours after they'd started. Now she had an excuse. She had to help clean up her house, didn't she?

"Hey, Holly," Colette said, when Holly peeked into the almost empty party room. "This is Kelly. She's a friend of my mom's." Colette glanced at the empty trash bags in Holly's hands. "Oh good. I forgot those. Kelly stayed to help me clean up."

"Hey, Kelly." Holly made mental notes. Kelly was younger than Rachel but older than Colette. "Did you all have a good meeting?"

"Well, we did. We needed to sort out all this madness with Will being arrested."

"Everyone except me has decided that the poisoning was accidental," Colette said. "Something with the food. But in my opinion, the police would not have arrested Will if they thought for one minute Jordan's death was an accident."

Holly didn't say anything in front of Kelly about what Amanda had revealed about cause of death being a holiday plant that Jordan had ingested, but her research convinced her that if the holiday plant was mistletoe, which she still didn't know for sure, the poisoning had not been accidental. Who bit off a hunk of mistletoe for fun? No. Someone had pulverized the plant and added it to Jordan's food or drink. At least, that was Holly's working theory. She was almost tempted to go out with Sam one more time just to test it on him, see if he'd tell her anything. But no. She couldn't.

She really wanted to know what everyone in the club had said, how they'd said it, and what their body language had betrayed.

Holly held up a half bottle of wine. "Should we finish this?" she said.

"Sure," Kelly said.

"I have to get back to the kids."

Holly poured two glasses of wine and handed one to Kelly before she could escape. "That's fine, Colette.

Go ahead, I've got this."

"You sure?"

"Absolutely."

"Okay then, see you at the office tomorrow." Colette left with a full bag of garbage, hauling it out back to the Dumpster for Holly.

"Have a seat?" Holly said.

Kelly sat down and kicked off her shoes. "Oh, does that feel good. Honey, you get to my age and you really can't wear heels without paying hell."

Holly didn't think Kelly looked a day over forty, but she knew better than to throw numbers around any women remotely older than she was. "I like heels, but then, I'm short," Holly said.

"And young," Kelly added.

"I'm curious," Holly said. "You mentioned almost all of you in the club think Will is innocent. Who thinks he's guilty?"

"Besides Colette? Nobody. She's got a blind spot where Will is concerned. He was a player in high school and he still kind of is, so she holds it against him. I think there is some former crush involved there."

"Yeah, you could be right."

"It's totally normal when you're just divorced to think of the one who got away. First thing divorced people do is look up old flames on Facebook. I have heard stories!"

"I have too. And I've only been out of high school, well, seven years now. I guess that's a chunk of time when I think about it."

"Not really. Try twenty years. Or forty."

There was no way Kelly was almost sixty. Unless she had a face lift. Did people in Blue Lake actually get face lifts? Holly studied Kelly's face. There were crow's feet around her eyes and some creases around her mouth, faint lines she could hardly see.

"You have not been out of school for forty years," Holly said.

"Well, no. Not quite. But there was this couple, you could see it happening on their posts—always hearts instead of likes. First one to leave a comment for the other. Him gushing about how beautiful she was for all the world to see, and she acting like a coy schoolgirl. They got married!"

"That might make a really interesting piece for the *Trib*. Maybe a Valentine's Day feature. Facebook Flames Reignite. You okay with me using your idea?"

"Sure."

"So I talked to India the other day, and she told me she used to date Jordan. So sad."

"Well, right. Before Phoebe. I think Jordan and Phoebe broke up but maybe were getting back together again. So India and Jordan were before all that."

"Did India break up with Jordan, or did he dump her?"

"I'm not really sure. All I know is India's been with them all. Jordan, Will, Patrick, and Quinn. Not necessarily in that order."

"Was Jordan, ah, was he a nice guy?"

"Not to speak ill of the dead, but not really. The reason Phoebe broke up with him the first time was because he showed around some photos she'd made for him. You know, nudes. At least that's what I heard. But then why would she get back together with him? And I have to say, they looked pretty cozy that night. Well, until he died."

"Wow."

"Yeah. Frankly most of these members fuck like rabbits. It's a bit incestuous. But you know, we do help each other out, too."

The next day at work, Holly checked with Colette about Kelly's story of out-of-control sex romps among the divorced people. "Not that I know of." Colette laughed. "I mean, not as bad as she makes it sound. Not picking up that vibe at all so far." Colette stopped for a minute and thought. "If Jordan did have photos or video or whatever of Phoebe, and he showed it to the guys, why would she get back with him?"

"Yeah, it seems weird." Holly didn't understand women who sent photos like that or people who made sex tapes, but she knew it was pretty common.

"Why do you care? You're not going to print this stuff, are you?"

"No. I only print the facts. But I am curious, just like everyone else." She didn't tell Colette about her mistletoe research. It was only a guess. Probably because of that pamphlet at Bob's house. It could have been any holiday plant. Maybe she could ask India for a list of the plants she'd used to decorate Will's house. Then she could research all of them. Process of elimination. But then India might figure out why Holly wanted to know. And Holly couldn't betray Amanda.

"So there were five of you last night. Wasn't there a sixth the night Jordan died? With Will, seven. And the caterers made nine. Then Jordan was ten. That's my head count anyway."

Holly really wanted to write down anything Colette might say, might know without knowing she knew it. She wanted to eliminate suspects. She wanted to believe the death was accidental food poisoning. But then why would Sam insist it was murder? Was he just an incompetent cop? The whole thing felt sloppy. She liked order. She wanted to organize it in her mind. She wanted to know what had really happened that night.

Colette counted on her fingers. "At first it was kind of a blur to me, but I've thought about it so many times." She held up four fingers. "Me, Will, Patrick, Quinn." She opened her hand to include the thumb. "Kelly." She started in on the next hand. "Phoebe—she quit the club after Jordan died. Sent us all an email saying she couldn't handle it." So that was six, and in a flash she used up the rest of her fingers: "Jordan, India, Two Sisters."

"Okay. Ten." Holly felt more organized but still felt a bit spooked about having the club upstairs from where she lived. She tried not to think about that and just go with the facts. "So do you think that's why everyone in the club believes it was accidental poisoning? Because it makes them feel safe?"

"And because nobody can believe Will, their friend, the guy who started the whole Fun Divorce Club, would actually be capable of murder. But I think he is. The cops got the right guy, and I for one feel safer with him off the streets."

Holly wasn't convinced. She called Amanda to see if she wanted to get a drink after work. Holly named a bar in the next town, one they'd been to before, that had a two-for-one Happy Hour and not-awful white wine. It was west of Blue Lake Woods, so they wouldn't be as likely to be overheard. Amanda said yes, if Holly could leave work at a reasonable hour.

They spent a good half hour sipping their wine and

talking about Blue Lake Woods. Holly told Amanda about her dream of owning a condo, and how she would decorate it, and maybe take cooking lessons, too. Amanda cheered her on and promised to share her favorite go-to recipes. Holly asked about Amanda's kids. Each had their own special storyline. Amanda could make new braces or a failed college course sound like high drama, so Holly enjoyed herself as she caught up with what was new this week. Finally, Holly asked when the toxicology report was going to be released.

"I don't know," Amanda said. "Maybe it already has." Then she slapped her hand over her mouth and looked around. They were sitting at the bar, and nobody else was there. Small town bars were great that way in winter. The bartender was so not paying attention, Holly had to clink her wine glass on the bar to get them another round and give Amanda a chance to calm down.

They silently waited for the fresh glasses of Chardonnay and for the bartender to retreat to the other end of the long bar, where he stuck his nose in his newspaper.

"You cannot print this," Amanda said. "But I know Two Sisters are worried. Have they been bugging you, too?"

Holly nodded, although the sisters hadn't called her, not even once. But she was bugged, to put it in Amanda's words. Only what was actually bugging her was not knowing the cause of death even though Will was in jail under suspicion of murder.

"The poison was ingested. Two hours before death, so before dinner," Amanda admitted under the influence.

"Could it have been in an appetizer?" Holly wondered out loud.

"No, see, that's the thing. I think this must be from the autopsy. The coroner's report, maybe. I don't get to see all that stuff, but the chief talks to me sometimes. So the contents of the stomach at time of death, just the punch that was served and the poison. No food at all."

"I wish I could report that. I mean, it's a fact," Holly said.

"Yeah, but, I think the chief wants to keep that idea of the poisoning being maybe accidental afloat, at least until after the holidays." Amanda made a good point.

"Then why arrest Will?" Holly wondered.

"I just don't know." Amanda sipped her drink.

"Okay, well, I want to do my job and report the facts, but I can see why maybe this should stay quiet until after the holidays. But it only makes sense if Will is the actual killer, because it would be unfair to the community to have a murderer on the loose." Holly paused, then said, "I don't think Will did it."

"Neither do I. But still. I could lose my job for confiding in you. So please, please do not print this," Amanda pleaded.

They drained their second glasses, which was their limit unless Amanda's husband was driving. Holly put down a twenty, more than enough for their Happy Hour drinks and a generous tip.

"Amanda, when I tell you it's off the record, it's off the record." She put her hand over Amanda's.

"I know, kiddo. Hey, how's Bob?"

So Holly told her the latest non-news.

****

Sam kept calling for another date. Bob didn't call.

101

He didn't text. She was a little lonely so it would have been easy to say yes to Sam, about as easy as it would have been to say yes to the book deal the agent had offered. But somehow there was a nagging feeling that Bob was right, that Uncle Eddie and Aunt Courtney were right, that Lily had the right to her own privacy and Holly should not meddle. And she should not date Sam to pump him for information. It was different with Amanda. They were friends. Amanda knew her secrets were safe with Holly. And Holly felt like some of the stuff Amanda said just built up inside her and she needed a safe place to spill.

Then Will was let out of jail. A murder suspect on the loose? How did that even happen? Sure, he was rich. But really? The evidence pointing to him as murderer must not be that compelling. Holly decided to take a walk down the beach. Maybe Will would want to give an interview, tell his side of the story.

Holly wanted the scoop, and she was willing to risk her life to get it. Well, not really. If she thought for a moment Will was guilty, she would never have put on her coat and boots and faced the freezing snowy beach.

She had good reason to believe he was innocent. Kelly had said Jordan had partnered with Will in a business venture involving the country club and a horse farm. Apparently, horses cost a lot of money to maintain, and Will wanted Jordan's steady influx of cash. So, why would he kill his new partner? It just didn't add up.

Also, there was her gut telling her Colette had overreacted due to an ancient crush gone bad combined with divorce blues, and Sam had wanted to make an arrest so he could be a hero and the town could breath easy during the holidays. Also, she really wanted the scoop. She stood on the beach in front of Will's house, looking into the big windows and the lit room within. It was getting dark so early these days. She'd left the house before five o'clock and already darkness, plus another inch of snow, had fallen.

Will answered the beach door right away. He didn't look like he'd been in jail at all. Not even a hipster beard. His perfectly angled jaw set hard, his muscular arms crossed tight, Will was the picture of noncompliance. She smiled. She'd had a tough time with interviews before—look at her first one with Bob. And that had turned out okay. Well, until it didn't. But Will would be different.

"I came to see if you wanted to tell your side of the story."

She hoped he wouldn't slam the door in her face. The look of hopeful trust that softened his features for a second before his scowl wiped it away melted her heart a little bit. Not in a romantic way. He was too old. At least thirty-five. But still good-looking. No wonder Colette had been so flustered by him.

When Will continued to study her as the snow made a shawl on her shoulders, she smiled wider. "Invite me in?"

He reluctantly moved aside. "How can I be sure you won't do a hatchet job on me? I know Colette thinks I killed Jordan."

She didn't have to ask how he knew that. Small towns. Everyone knew everything all the time. "I don't think you did it." And Holly explained her reasons to Will while she took off her coat and shook it onto the beautiful rug protecting his wood floor. She hadn't gotten a good look in this room when she'd been here the night of the murder. There was the grand piano, although there was no mistletoe, no trace of greenery, not even a tree, gracing the space. She supposed the police had taken it all as evidence. She hung her coat on a row of hooks artfully fastened to a length of driftwood beside the door and toed off her snowy boots, being careful not to get her wool socks wet.

"Make yourself comfortable," Will said, his tone deeply ironic.

"Thanks," she said, walking over to the sofa and plopping down, settling her purse with recorder and notebook at her feet. "I'm staying just down the beach at Blue Heaven."

"Yeah, I heard. Holly Fass, cub reporter."

"Only reporter," she said. Star reporter, she wanted to say.

"Does Colette know you're here?"

"Yep. She knows I think she's full of crap about you doing it. She knows my reasons. But I had a feeling it wasn't you from the very beginning."

"Why? You don't know me."

"I'm not really sure. Well, most people didn't believe you did it. He was your new partner. You're a good guy. Upstanding citizen. A credit to the community. Just Sam and Colette seem to think you did it."

"Well, thanks. And for the record, I didn't do it," he said.

She took this as an invitation to pull out her recorder. She held it up with her index finger on record. He nodded. She pushed and set it on the highly polished coffee table. She wondered who'd cleaned his house while he was in jail. Of course, that would not be a good question to lead with. She hadn't been at all sure Will would talk to her, and she had decided so quickly after he was released to come down here to see him that she hadn't had time to prepare. Not specifically. But she'd been living and breathing the case since the night after Thanksgiving. She could wing it.

"So I thought I would start with the background of the case, including your new partnership with Jordan, which is probably a pretty strong motive NOT to murder him."

Will nodded. "That would be okay."

"So, what evidence did they have against you?"

"I'm not sure I should answer that. I'm still 'a person of interest.' "

"Oh! I didn't know. Well, maybe you can check with your lawyer? I'll wait." Holly knew she needed fresh meat to feed the townsfolk. The flimsy (it must have been if they'd had to let him go, right?) evidence against Will would be an excellent score.

"I'm not calling him. I've seen enough of that guy in the last forty-eight hours. I just want some peace."

"And maybe a Christmas tree?" Holly figured she could wheedle the info out of Will another way.

He actually laughed. "You want a drink?"

Oh, that was not a good idea. She was on the job. But it might help him relax. And talk more. She didn't have to write anything down, just let the recorder do its work. "Okay."

He brought back two glasses of wine, one red, one white. "Which do you prefer?" he asked.

She took the white. Red stained her teeth. She sipped, cautioning herself to go slow. That was the good thing about red wine, she drank it very slowly. But she knew guys preferred red if they drank wine at all. So she'd made the sacrifice.

"So what's so funny about a Christmas tree?" She'd let him get at least half the glass down him before she'd pounce with her pet theory about the evidence against him.

"It's the last thing on my mind right now," he said.

"But you had one. Colette said you had the house all decorated. And I spoke to India. She mentioned she'd done your house for the party. By the way, India was quite vocal in her support of you. She wouldn't even entertain the idea that you were guilty."

Will seemed to mellow. He drank deep and threw another log on the fire.

"I've been reading your coverage of the case. So far, I have to admit you've been more than fair."

"Just the facts. They speak pretty plainly." She eyed his wine. Now or never. She reached for her own glass and took a sip for courage. She had to know the truth. "For example, India said she hung mistletoe above the piano. And a source tells me the poison was a holiday plant. India didn't mention any other plants like that, with berries. I mean, it's going to come out soon, right? The police suspected you'd muddled the mistletoe and slipped it into Jordan's drink?"

Before Will could answer, his phone rang.

They both looked at it, buzzing on the coffee table next to her glass of wine. Will reached over and declined the call. "That phone has been ringing since I walked in the door. It stopped when you got here, but I should have known people would not leave me alone." He drained his glass of wine. "They mean well." He got up to grab the bottle of red off the piano. She really didn't think he should use his pretty piano for a bar, but she wasn't going to offer that opinion.

"You know, Will, I've never thought you did it. I would never have come here if I believed you killed Jordan. My problem is I think the killer is still out there. I'm not sure why the police even arrested you if it was the mistletoe. I mean, anyone could buy the same batch at the Farmer's Market. I bought some!"

Will didn't say anything. He poured a generous amount of red into his glass and looked with disapproval at her mostly full one. Then the phone rang again. After a quick look, he declined the call.

"After you were arrested, I did a little digging," Holly said. "I thought maybe the police found an oak tree on your property with mistletoe growing on it. But did you know mistletoe doesn't grow in Michigan? It's more a southern plant. And not all varieties are poisonous. I bought some from the Farmer's Market, and they said they didn't think it was a poisonous variety, but to be safe, not to eat it. Still, anyone who bought any mistletoe could have added it to Jordan's drink—I heard you had a potent punch that would disguise the taste."

The more Will drank, the more his face relaxed. He nodded. "I don't see why you can't print that."

"It's all conjecture at this point." She didn't mention what Amanda had told her.

"But then why are you writing it down?"

Holly was embarrassed. She put her notebook away and let the recorder get the rest of the story.

"I will be printing the full story at some point. I just want to be ready. You know?"

"So who's your main suspect?"

"Someone at the party that night. So that narrows down the suspect pool. India decorated your house; she had access. Not that I suspect her. The real murderer would want to implicate you, too, right?" She began to dig into her thought process, all the things she had held back from print so far. "Poisoning is not a spur-of-the-moment crime. All the murderer had to do was put the poison in a little container, then bring it to the party and spike Jordan's drink. It's not like it was an accident."

Will finished his second glass. Poured another. "But what if whoever did it didn't mean to kill Jordan? Maybe they meant the drink for someone else, but it got switched somehow?" Will stopped speaking abruptly. He must have realized he was painting himself into a bit of a corner. "I mean, that could be why the police were so sure I did it even though it was Jordan who died. But don't print that."

"No, I won't," Holly promised. She realized Will was right. Maybe the murderer wanted to kill someone else with that drink. But who? And why?

The phone rang again, and she slipped her recorder into her purse, a little relieved. Time to go.

"I need to take this," Will said.

"I'm just leaving." Holly stood and walked over to the door. Gosh, this was a big room. She felt a little wobbly from the wine as she pulled on her boots and shot her arms through the sleeves of her coat.

****

"You have a date for the Sleigh Bell Ball?" Colette asked.

Holly not only did not have a date, she did not know what Colette was talking about. She tossed her empty coffee cup and looked up from the story on Will she was polishing before sending to Colette. She had yet to tell Colette she'd barged in on Will and gotten a scoop yesterday.

Well, not a factual scoop, but at least an interview professing his innocence. And she could write about his partnership with Jordan. But she wouldn't put forth any further theories about the poison or how it was administered.

"What is a Sleigh Bell Ball?"

"A charity thing. Mom must not have gotten a chance to tell you about it. We'll go together. I don't have a date, either. And you need to cover it for the paper anyway. What are you working on?"

Holly felt jittery and not just from the three cups of coffee she'd had so far this morning. "I scored an interview with Will."

"What?! I didn't think he'd let you in the house! Let me read it!"

Holly gave up on the polish. That's what editors were for. She sent it to Colette's laptop as she summarized the meeting the night before.

"You're amazing, Holly. I mean it."

Whew. She had been worried Colette would go all maternal on her, warning her she could be next on Will's hit list. But then, even if Will had killed Jordan, people were pretty safe for now. He wouldn't dare kill again with the police watching him so closely.

Holly looked at the files for "Sleigh Bell Ball" and began doing prep for that story. She didn't know when this party was being held, but it didn't matter. She had zero future plans until her parents got to town a few days before Christmas. Which was weeks away still.

Well, twelve days. So the ball was probably this coming weekend. And she hadn't shopped yet. She hadn't even started a list.

****

By the end of the week, Holly had filed five stories and finished her Christmas list. She'd even managed to buy a dress for the ball with a matching burgundy velvet coat. The coat was lined and long, which she would need as the Sleigh Bell Ball featured those famous Blue Lake sleigh rides. And Holly would need to take one of them, so she could write about it. Probably, though, without Bob.

Just thinking about Bob, and the fact that he might be at the event tonight, compelled her to add a third layer of mascara to her eyelashes.

Colette beeped the horn of her mom's Jeep just as Holly was swapping out the contents of her bag for something a little more formal. She didn't bother with her recorder or notebook. She had all the facts, now she just needed atmosphere. And that she could remember. Especially if Bob happened to be there.

But the first person she saw after they arrived was not Bob. It was Will. Colette stiffened next to Holly.

"My fan club," Will said. But he smiled when he said it. Holly couldn't tell about him. Was he teasing Colette because he knew she was afraid of him? Was he teasing her because she'd written up her interview with him with objectivity she didn't quite feel? What people didn't know was that her notebook contained every wild theory that woke her in the middle of the night. It was her safe place where she didn't have to stick to the facts, didn't have to hide other people's secrets, and could indulge in the kind of thinking that dear old Lily

White was doing as a private investigator.

Then Holly saw Bob across the room, talking to his brother and Eva.

Colette said something, but Holly missed her remark because she'd been staring at Bob. Then Will replied. "Nobody thinks I did it except you and Sam Carpenter. And I thought you were my friends."

Colette had no reply to that, but Will had stalked off anyway.

"I don't think he did it, Colette."

"So you say."

"No, well, I mean, he could have done it. But so could Phoebe. Or India. We need to find out if those nude photos were real or just rumor."

"Why don't we ask Will?" Because Will had reappeared with two glasses of white wine for them.

"Ask me what?" he said.

"Did Jordan show you nude photos, or maybe a video, like a sex tape, of Phoebe?"

Will choked a little on his drink. Something clear and on the rocks.

Patrick and Quinn appeared just then, and Colette introduced the other Fun Divorce Club guys to Holly. Holly repeated her question so that they all could answer.

"Watch out, guys. She's a reporter. She'll get you drunk and then get you to spill all your secrets."

Just then, Holly saw India sitting at one of the tables further into the room with another woman. Phoebe.

"Come on," Holly said. "It's a rumor. Just tell us, off the record. Did Phoebe send a topless photo or a video, maybe a sex tape, to Jordan?"

One of the guys—she didn't know which one was Patrick and which one was Quinn—said, "Well, yeah, there was a video, not a sex tape, just Phoebe doing a little fantasy number. Topless only. Pretty tame." Holly did not want to ask what a fantasy number was. And if it was tame, then what was racy? She didn't want to know. "Only the guys saw it, but it was a long time ago." The others nodded agreement. They looked a little bored by it all.

The band started playing a song from sometime before any of them had been born. Older couples went out on the floor and slow danced. It was kind of sweet to see the ladies with their silver hair in updos hanging on to their husbands so they didn't fall over in their heels, probably only brought out for occasions like this.

"Let's just enjoy the night and not think about the murder, okay?"

Holly was still trying to figure out which guy was Patrick and which one was Quinn. It probably didn't matter. Poison was a woman's murder weapon of choice. And the ladies, especially Phoebe, had a better motive than the guys for wanting Jordan dead. She didn't say what she was thinking—that something like a topless video posted online could be used in a custody fight. She wondered how much child support Phoebe's husband paid. It wouldn't be the first time a man would fight for custody just so he wouldn't have to pay as much support. Phoebe might be a good person, but sometimes good people did unfortunate things. Even bad things. And Holly really believed that a mother would do almost anything to keep her kids. Now she just had to figure out a way to talk to the women in the club about their children and their exes.

Holly's eyes kept straying toward Bob's table all through dinner. She checked him out covertly during the silent auction. When the band started up again after dinner, he still didn't ask anybody to dance. That was a good sign, wasn't it? On the other hand, he hadn't looked back at her, not even a glance, not even once.

"Okay, I'm going to get on that list for a sleigh ride, and then can we please go home?" When Colette made a vague reply, Holly wished she'd brought her own car. This gala was putting her in a seriously bad mood. She might as well brood in private.

****

"I'm not going on a sleigh ride," Bob said.

"I already paid for you. It's for a good cause," Eva said.

Toys for kids. Bob knew. His family adopted several kids every year, but so many little ones needed winter coats and boots, not to mention toys under the tree. He sucked it up. Eva was pregnant after all. She couldn't be expected to go on a sleigh ride on yet another snowy night. At least it wasn't bitterly cold. Not like it would be in January.

"Fine. I'm going to do it now though before the rush."

Bob set down his coffee and went to queue up for the sleigh ride. There was only one other person in the line. Holly. She turned around and looked right at him. Caught him scowling at her. Looked like she might cry.

Maybe she wasn't so terrible after all. She didn't end up writing the book. She'd thought better of it. And she had good qualities. Plus he missed her. She was a really good kisser. He smiled, and she smiled back at him.

Chapter Ten

Holly was super glad she'd bought the new coat. Not because it kept her warm, but because she wanted to look her best for Bob. The way he smiled at her, so tender and sincere, made the cold clear night seem full of possibility.

The driver helped them into the sleigh, then put a wool blanket over their laps. Something about being under a cover together made Holly warm in the cold night. She watched the breath puffing out of the horse's nostrils, the stars shining in the sky. What was happening to her? She needed to keep her grip on reality. It was a sleigh ride, nothing more. Then Bob put his arm around her and pulled her a little bit closer.

As the driver took his seat in front of them, he gave the reins a jingle. Holly felt her heart jingle too. With Bob next to her, she had all the warmth she needed. It was as if she could feel his body heat through all the layers that separated them. She felt deliciously alive. And something more, like she had a superpower. The power to feel his skin beneath all those layers.

"I've missed you," Bob said as they glided through the snow.

"I've missed you, too," she said.

The moon was out. She could see his eyes in its glow. He looked so deeply into her eyes that she felt a hook, a connection, within. What was that? All of the unfamiliar sensations almost overwhelmed her, but with Bob by her side, she was not afraid to feel new things. She snuggled more deeply into his embrace. He encircled her in his arms.

The night was still as they moved through the darkness that wrapped around them like a cloak. They were the only animation in a silent world. The hush surrounding the snowy trees as they took a path through a clearing felt almost holy. Holly was deeply content. This felt right in a way she couldn't explain. She felt almost like a kid again, out getting a ride on a sled in the snow. She stuck out her tongue to catch a flake.

Bob laughed. "What are you doing?"

"This night is so delicious I want to eat it."

He touched her face with his glove, turned her toward him, and kissed her. She wondered if they were out of sight of the country club's many large windows. Then she got lost in him and didn't care anymore who saw them.

"Whoa!"

The sleigh plowed through a big drift of snow, showering them with the fluffy white flakes. Way to put a damper on that kiss. She brushed the snow off her face.

"Did you drive here?" Bob asked.

"No. I came with Colette."

"I was going to leave after the sleigh ride."

"Me too."

"Does Colette want to stay? Because I can drive you home. Or we could go out for a drink."

"Or you could drive me home and I could make us a drink. I never did get to make you a hot chocolate. It is one of the few recipes I've perfected." Holly wondered if this time, Bob would stay. It had not felt quite right before. But something about this night said tonight was magical.

The snow softly fell. She snuggled into Bob's embrace, feeling like she never wanted to leave. All of her worries, all of her cares, melted away. The book contract, the condo, even the murder…all of it melted like snow on her tongue when Bob kissed her again.

Back at the country club, she and Bob quickly said their goodbyes. Neither of them could wait to be alone, then out of the car, then out of their layers and into her house. Bob started a fire in the front room while Holly melted chocolate into milk in the kitchen. Her heart would not stop pounding. It had been a really long time since she'd been with someone, but this felt right. She poured the steaming chocolate into mugs and added a glop of whipped cream to each.

They sat in front of the fire, so close to each other their legs entwined. Soon the hot drinks were forgotten as they kissed again. She could not get enough of his sweet lips, his hot mouth. The fire popped and blazed, but it couldn't warm Holly more than Bob's kisses did. Her body arched toward his. Heart met heart, both madly beating.

Bob dragged his tongue down her neck to her throat. She felt his warm breath on her skin as he tugged down one shoulder of her velvet dress, licking his way across her collarbone. His fingers found her breast under her dress, and he rubbed sweetly at the silk of her bra until her entire body ached and a moan escaped. She was so far gone she wasn't even embarrassed getting vocal on him. "Ohh, yess," she said and he laughed low, turning it into a growl as he scooped her nipple out of its cup and flicked the hardening nub with his tongue. She gave in willingly to the rush she felt zing through her, not even caring that he was totally crushing her dress.

Before he had her half undressed, she pushed him a little off. Huh, how had he ended up on top of her, half reclined on the sofa? "Let's go into the bedroom," she said, wanting more privacy than the front room windows—without any kind of curtain or blind—allowed. Bob moved off her, and she felt a breeze on her skin despite the warm fire burning in the hearth, and in her. She smiled at him, feeling shy. She tugged her dress up to cover herself a little better and then led him into the bedroom. She took her dress off and put it on a hanger. Bob almost simultaneously had his hands all over her, touching, rubbing, and kissing her everywhere. They weren't even on the bed yet! At this rate, they wouldn't make it to the bed!

Bob scooped her into his arms and moved her over to the mattress, laying her down on the duvet like she was a priceless item. He stepped back and looked straight into her eyes as he unzipped his pants and ripped at the buttons on his shirt. She watched him undress. It was the most erotic thing ever. He noticed her noticing and appreciating, stripped every last stitch off. Then he moved over her and did the same to her. This, this was what she'd wanted in the sleigh, to feel his skin against her skin, to let their heat explode, to open to him and feel his thrust, just rough enough.

He rode her right over a cliff and she went willingly. Things got very vocal on her end, but she felt like it was okay to show him who she really was. She trusted him. When finally they were finished, she lay in the circle of his arms and felt contentment settle over her. She hoped this meant they were dating again.

After a few minutes, Bob whispered in her ear, "Let's spend Christmas together."

"Okay."

Bob ran his hand down her body, still warm from their lovemaking. "You are so beautiful, Holly."

She wasn't, but it was nice of him to think so. Had there ever been a more perfect night? If there had been, she couldn't remember it right now. Right now felt like it might be as good as anything could get without exploding. And she had kind of exploded. Twice. She sighed and settled more deeply into his arms.

"I'm glad you gave up the book deal," he said. "I knew you were a good person, Holly." He kissed her on the cheek, but by then she already felt like she'd been dumped with cold water.

Should she tell him the truth? What was the truth? She forgot. Her mind felt numb and wiped clean. She needed to think. Beside her, Bob let out a loud snore. Oh man. She might have whiplash. A minute ago, she'd have been happy for him to spend the night. Now, all she wanted to do was run into her closet and hide inside her velvet dress.

She gently extricated herself from Bob. She padded over to the closet and pulled her robe off its hook, then took herself out into the living room. The fire had turned to dying embers. She poked at it half-heartedly, then took her mug of chocolate into the kitchen. Zapped it in the microwave.

She always thought better with chocolate. She pulled the can of whipped cream out of the fridge and gave her drink another shot. She had a feeling she was going to need it.

"Hey." Bob had come so silently out of the bedroom she hadn't heard him approach. "Should I put another log on the fire?"

"Ah, well, yeah, no, I don't know." She shrugged, confused. Bob took this as a yes and loaded another log on the fire.

"What about the dogs?" Holly asked.

"Dogs?" Bob said. "Oh, the dogs. I forgot about them." He raked his bedhead, making him if possible even more sexy. "Guess I need to go and see to them." Bob kissed her again, the casual kiss of a boyfriend going home.

Once she heard his car start, Holly breathed. She'd figure this out. It wasn't that complicated. She had a choice. She could choose Bob or an independent life with a book contract and a condo of her own.

What would choosing Bob look like? A tiny flat in town above one of the restaurants or stores? A job she loved but that would hardly pay the bills and would probably in the near future be completely online and thus pay even less?

Chapter Eleven

Holly had no answers to the Bob problem, so she decided to visit Ernie. It had been three weeks since his heart attack. He was home and feeling up to company, or so Rachel had texted Holly. Holly texted back asking if she could stop by and bring lunch. Rachel answered with one word, all in caps: PLEASE.

"I'm seeing your mom and Ernie for lunch today." Holly talked to Colette over the clatter of her keyboard. "Can I bring you something back?"

"Oh, what are you guys having for lunch?"

"Uncle Eddie is making chili. I can have him box up a bowl for you."

"That would be so great. I've got to get these Christmas letters edited. It is amazing how many people want to share how gifted their children are and how well their portfolios are doing with the town this time of year."

"Haha, I do not envy you. I can hardly read the ones from my relatives!" Holly snagged her coat. "I'm going by the bakery too, to get some corn bread and dessert. Want anything special? Something sweet?"

"Oh, could you get a dozen oatmeal chocolate cookies?" Colette thought the oatmeal made these cookies better for her children.

Holly just nodded. "Will do."

First, Holly stopped by the florist and got a

bouquet. She wasn't sure if it was more to cheer up Ernie or Rachel. Then she stopped for Uncle Eddie's famous chili, said a quick hello to her uncle, and headed to the bakery. The sisters were both in, one behind the counter and the other in the back, pulling peach pies out of the oven. Holly's order was boxed up and waiting.

"Hey, Holly. Have you heard anything more about the murder? Like where the poison came from?"

Holly knew the sisters had been worried about their business taking a dive after the poisoning was reported. The baking sister came out front to hear Holly's reply, which just proved that they were more worried than they should be. Why couldn't the police release the full details? Unless they didn't really know. But Amanda had said it was a holiday plant.

"It was NOT food poisoning. But the exact type of poison has not be made public."

"I never saw that in print. That it was definitely not food poisoning." One of the sisters said. The one with red hair.

"Sorry, they call you Red, right?"

"Yeah."

Holly looked around the small cozy bakery. The back room was bigger than the storefront, which had bread racks and cookies and pies in a glass-front cabinet, and a cash register and two little tables under the front window. They had a coffee pot, but Two Sisters was not really an eat-in establishment. Mostly people sat down to wait for their orders to be boxed. Maybe they sampled a piece of pie and had a cup of coffee while they waited. Nobody but Holly and the sisters were here now.

"I have the information on good authority, but no,

it hasn't been made public yet."

"Why not?"

"My source could be compromised if I printed that information. Like you, I really thought it would be public knowledge by now."

"Amanda," said the blonde sister. "She's the source!"

Holly didn't deny it. "Have you guys lost any business because of the murder?"

"No, but we were seriously worried."

"Well, don't be. In fact, I'll run a little story online about how well Ernie is doing and how he dined on your pie and corn bread this afternoon."

"Oh, would you? Thanks so much."

"You want to add anything about your holiday hours? Specials?" Holly got out her recorder as the sisters began to spin visions of sugar plums. She could feel herself gaining weight just listening to them.

At Ernie's a little later, Holly noticed that Ernie looked healthier than Rachel, who looked exhausted. Ernie beamed at the bags of food, blushed at Holly's kiss on the cheek, and sat with his Sudoku book while Holly and Rachel went into his kitchen to dish up lunch. Rachel seemed to know her way around Ernie's kitchen, pulling out bowls and spoons and butter.

"Is it too early for a glass of wine?" Rachel asked.

"Go ahead. But I have to write a story today. I'm going to just post a little something on seeing Ernie. Can I snap a photo with my phone, do you think?"

"Sure, sure. Good idea." Rachel went right ahead and poured herself a glass of wine. Holly noticed she didn't ask Ernie if he'd like anything to drink. Poor Rachel was probably a bit weary of nursing. Anyone would be. Plus Ernie's house was dark. Even the kitchen had walnut cabinets and earth-toned blinds over the window. His appliances were avocado green. His table was from the colonial period. Or would that be faux-colonial? Circa 1969, anyway.

"I saw a friend of yours the other day." Holly told Rachel about her conversation with Kelly. "Something she said made me think Phoebe might be a suspect. Something about her ex, a video, and child custody."

"Ah, support. Yeah, Colette had a bit of an issue with that, too. Her ex thought since the kids didn't live in Florida anymore, so he didn't get to see them, then he shouldn't have to pay. A judge told him different, but still. These guys can be weird about paying support."

"So, what do you think? I don't know much about Phoebe. She dropped out of the Fun Divorce Club after the murder, so I never met her."

"Well, surely the police are handling things, Holly. But you're doing a good job on that story. Very balanced. I really liked the interview with Will. I just can't believe he'd kill someone."

"I agree, although I am doing my best to report objectively."

"And you're doing well with that. I'm really proud of you. Colette praises you to the skies."

"I couldn't do it without her."

"I'm sure you could."

"No, really. It's too much with the business end. I'm just a writer."

Holly wanted to talk more about Phoebe, but Rachel was already calling Ernie over to the table. After they settled in and pigged out, Holly went over to the countertop to cut the pie.

"Peach is my favorite," Ernie said.

"I know. The Sisters told me you buy one most every week."

"Too bad the doctor told me to lay off the vanilla ice cream," Ernie remarked. He perked up with Holly placed his pie in front of him.

"I don't know about that pie crust," Rachel said.

"Ease off, woman." Ernie dug into his pie, crust and all.

Rachel huffed.

"I'm sorry," Holly silently mouthed to Rachel.

"Ernie, Holly and I are going out tonight with Kelly."

This was news to Holly. But welcome news.

"Oh?" Ernie lay down his fork.

"You'll be fine. And I've got to get out of the house, or I'll go stir crazy."

"Of course, dear. You go right ahead. Where are you gals heading to?"

"Fast Eddie's."

Holly had thus far avoided a night out at her uncle's bar. Sure, she stopped in for lunch once a week or so, and she got carry-outs for dinner sometimes. But she'd drawn the line at making a night of it at the only bar in town that was open winter nights. Somehow, she couldn't imagine drinking until she was fuzzy and dancing with strangers while her uncle looked on. And possibly reported it to her father. But heck, a girl's night? She could do that.

"What time should I pick you up, Rachel?"

"What time do you get off work?"

****

Kelly already had a table for them when Rachel and Holly got to Fast Eddie's. It was too early for a band, but they could get burgers. Her uncle Eddie made the best burgers in the entire state of Michigan.

Holly waited until they were on their second glass of wine before she brought up Phoebe. She looked around to see how close other patrons were, and then lowered her voice even though the juke box music should drown out her words. She didn't want to cause Phoebe any more pain over that whole Jordan and the porno tape thing, but she needed to know because it might be important to the larger story. Really important. So she asked if they'd heard anything.

"Holly is doing background on this story, so she can break the news the minute they find the actual killer." Rachel was being supportive, which Holly appreciated.

Holly guessed that was why she was interested. She hadn't really thought about why she wanted to know who killed Jordan before Rachel stated it in that way. She just knew she needed to know. Needed to establish the facts if she could. She was hoping the ladies would go on, especially with Rachel giving the tactical okay, and she was rewarded.

"Phoebe married a hometown boy. Still lives in town. Sees his kids every weekend," Kelly said.

Holly felt a shiver hit every bone of her spine, one at a time, like a hammer. If he still lived in town, his humiliation over a topless video of his ex and his anger that his children might see it might make him threaten to take the kids away from Phoebe. "What's his job? Could he leave town with the kids if he did get custody?"

"He's a plumber, and a good one, so yeah, he could go anywhere."

"He's not Stan the Plumber Man?!" Holly saw that guy's commercials on television all the time.

"One and the same." Rachel nodded, before snagging the waitress. "Another round, honey."

"Not for me. I'm driving," Holly said. In truth, she wanted to go home and make a phone call to a certain plumber. "And I've got an early morning."

"Honey, it's fine," Kelly said. "I can drive Rachel back to Ernie's. Now Rachel, what is going one with you and Ernie, anyway?"

****

Holly wished she had a broken faucet or something. But she didn't, so she called Stan on Sunday morning cold.

"You're the reporter for the paper," he said after she introduced herself.

"Yep. And I'd like you to just help me out with something."

"What?" Stan sounded doubtful.

"Well, it's not a plumbing problem, Stan."

He remained silent. Holly heard kids in the background. This was not easy.

"I heard about a compromising video of your ex-wife and got corroboration from a few people that the video does exist. The police have Jordan's phone, so I assume they've seen it, too."

"You can't print that!"

"No. I'm not going to. I just wanted to know the full story before it breaks elsewhere. The rumor mill is churning—I can't stop that."

"That stupid bitch." He said this low, probably so

his kids wouldn't hear.

"Okay, so I just have one question. Were you planning to use the video to get custody of your kids?"

"Jesus, who said that? I fucking hate this town."

"See, that's the thing. You could presumably get custody and leave a town you hate. People are going to connect those dots."

"My kids do not need to grow up in a town where their mother is known as the local skank." That was all the confirmation Holly needed. But Stan wasn't finished. "I never saw the video. Jordan never confirmed that he had it. We were going to meet the Monday after Thanksgiving."

"But he died Friday, before you could meet."

"Yep. Still, I know it exists. It's only a matter of time until someone puts it on online."

"I don't think so. Now that the police have it, it's not going anywhere. And nobody else has a copy."

"Well, I'm still pissed. I told her I was meeting Jordan. She seemed unconcerned, but she's a really good faker." His voice was louder now.

"I'm really sorry, Stan. I was hoping you'd tell me you had no intention to use the video to take the kids away from Phoebe."

"Are you saying—is someone putting it out there—"

She wasn't sure if he'd drawn the obvious conclusion or not. Well, maybe it was only obvious to her that Phoebe was only pretending to get back with Jordan so he would destroy the video. That maybe Phoebe had a much stronger motive than Will had to see Jordan dead. Or maybe Stan just didn't want to spell it out in front of the kids.

"I haven't heard anyone say anything except that the video does exist. And I'm not printing that."

"But nobody thinks—"

Again, he stopped before finishing his thought. Holly could finish it for him. "I haven't heard anyone accusing Phoebe of anything connected with Jordan's death."

"Because that would absolutely kill my kids."

"I get that."

"I've been reading your stories online. You seem like a fair person. Tell me this is not going into the papers."

"Absolutely not. I only print facts, not rumors."

"But you said people had admitted to seeing the video. Like who?"

"I can't reveal my sources, but I'm not going to print that information either. It isn't a story fit for a local paper." What she didn't say, but what she thought, was "not yet."

****

Holly felt sick after hanging up the phone. She made a cup of mint tea to settle her stomach and decided to take a bubble bath. Soaking, she thought of why she was upset. Two reasons. She felt grubby after talking to Stan. It really looked like Phoebe had a motive. At least more of a motive than Will. She certainly had opportunity. But what about means? Did the police even check her house for crushed mistletoe? Or some kind of container she used to transport the crushed plant to the party at Will's?

Her second reason for feeling a bit icky was that Bob had not called since the night of the Sleigh Bell Ball. They'd both been busy with work, but still. He could have called.

The minute she got out of the bath, wrinkled up like a prune, her phone rang. Not Bob. Sam. "I'm outside. Let me in."

"I'm not dressed," she started to say, but he'd already clicked off.

She threw on jeans and a sweater. The way he sounded, he just might bust in without waiting for her to unlock the door. What was he angry about? His frown did nothing to dispel the uncomfortable feeling that rushed back into her gut. She'd just gotten herself calmed down, and now here she was, all worked up again.

"What?" she said. He walked into the house right past her, heading for her quarters. "What the hell? Hello? Do you always just walk right into people's kitchens on Sunday afternoon?" Because the kitchen is where he stopped. He unzipped his police jacket, tossed it over a kitchen chair.

"Sit," he said.

"No," she said. Then she remembered they were on the same side, and she sat.

"Listen, Holly. You have gotten yourself into something here that you need to be aware of. I need you to stop interviewing murder suspects—leave this investigation to the police before you get hurt."

"What are you talking about?" But she knew. Stan the Plumber Man must have called the police.

"Come off it. How long has it been since you talked to Stan? An hour? And the interview you ran with Will—it's obvious you two have gotten cozy." Sam looked at her half-full coffee pot. "That hot?"

"No."

His eyes went to the microwave.

"Why? You want a cup of coffee?"

"Sure. If it's no trouble." He sat down at the table.

She got up. "Listen." She nuked the coffee, her back turned to him. "I wasn't going to print anything in my conversation with Stan. I just thought, you know, get the background in case the investigation takes a turn."

She set the mug of coffee down in front of him, taking her seat again. Maybe she could find out about the specific poison used. If she played nice. "Was Stan very upset?"

"Not with you. He's worried this will get out…"

"And his kids will be hurt." She finished his sentence. He nodded. "But I told him I wouldn't print that bit about the video."

"He said you had witnesses. People who had seen it. Who were they?"

Chapter Twelve

"I won't reveal my sources."

"This is a murder investigation, Holly. But never mind. Just tell me, was it Will?"

"You tell me something. Why are you keeping the type of poison a secret? It's freaking the Two Sisters out."

"They've got nothing to worry about."

"I know that and you know that, but they don't know that." Holly had run the piece about Ernie and Two Sisters. She hoped it helped as people got more and more curious about who had killed a hometown boy.

"What do you mean, you know that?"

"Well, it's just a guess." She would not out Amanda.

"Let's hear it."

"I'm thinking it was mistletoe poisoning."

"That's quite a stretch." Sam seemed annoyed.

"Not really." Holly thought back to the night at Bob's when she'd read about mistletoe poisoning. Her heart pinched. Why wasn't Bob calling? What if he stopped by and saw Sam's car? Would he think she had invited Sam over?

"Care to explain how you came to this conclusion?"

She told him about the pamphlet. She didn't tell

him about her research. "And then I saw India at the Farmer's Market, and she had all this mistletoe, and we got to talking, and she said she had decorated Will's place…and I kind of put one and one together."

"And came up with ten."

"Well, if it was food poisoning, you would have at least investigated the sisters, and you didn't."

"We questioned everyone."

"But if you know it was poison, you know what kind of poison."

"Not necessarily."

Holly kept silent. What did she know about it? Her phone beeped. Bob. "I have to take this," she said.

"You can call him back," Sam said.

"I don't know what else to say, Sam."

"Say you will stop questioning and interviewing the members of the Fun Divorce Club. Say you will keep yourself safe."

"I will. I promise." She was only promising to keep safe, not to stop doing her job. Which was to get as much information as she could about Jordan's murder. However she needed to get it.

"I mean it, Holly. There's trouble in this town. If the person who killed Jordan knows you're snooping around—Well. I don't have to paint you a picture."

"No. I get it. You're worried. That's sweet, really."

"It's my job."

"Okay, but we're friends, right?"

"We could have been more than friends, but it looks like you blew me off for the architect."

Okay, this was a little uncomfortable. "I'm sure you'll meet someone."

"You don't need to worry about me. I do all right."

"I'm sure you do."

"Well, then, why don't we go out again? We had fun, right?"

Holly remembered that date. It was just okay. How did you tell someone that they just didn't click? That they were lacking a kind of chemistry? If Sam didn't sense it, telling him would just hurt his feelings. He probably didn't get turned down much. He was super-handsome in a male model sort of way. Male models had never been her type. She didn't want a pretty boyfriend. Bob was handsome, but he wasn't pretty.

"I'm seeing Bob," she said.

"Yeah. Well, if that doesn't work out, you know my number." He got up, finally.

"I do. And thanks for your concern, Sam."

"No problem. Just—you know. Behave yourself."

"I will."

"Okay, then. I can see myself out."

****

She picked up her phone to call Bob, but it rang in her hand. "Hey," she said, expecting Bob. Thinking it was sweet that he'd called her back.

"Have you been watching this storm?"

Oh. Colette. "What storm?" Holly walked into the front room. The snow was coming down hard. Had it not stopped since yesterday? How many inches had accumulated?

"We've got a winter weather situation. Don't bother coming in. Just work from home. You need to write something we can post today. As soon as possible. Watch your weather app, and then call Luke Anderson. He does the snow removal in town."

"Will do." Holly clicked off and wondered if she

had time to call Bob. She sent him a text instead. "Sorry missed yr call. Weather story on front burner, will call after I write." She debated using her xo signoff but didn't. They hadn't mentioned love yet. She didn't want to be the first one to bring it up, even as an acronym. Did she love him? She thought she might be starting to. It really felt like it. She didn't want to say it though. It was like maybe a minute too soon.

She watched the weather on her phone and called Luke Anderson. He gave her the scoop on when he'd be scooping people out. Apparently, the next twenty-four hours would be a snow day for the kids of Blue Lake. "I'll have you plowed out for work tomorrow morning," Luke promised.

That was good enough. She wrote her story, sent it to Colette, and called Bob.

****

Bob got Holly's text. She was working, so he didn't feel too bad about working himself. He needed his preliminary design ready to show, like, yesterday. But he wasn't stressed about it; he was grateful. The new condo project had lit a fire under him. He was bursting with ideas and solutions to initial problems that he had to get down on the computer. He actually did some quick pencil sketches first just because there was so much detail he wanted to capture. It was easier to draw it all and then go back and refine it in his program.

He worked steadily at his loft window where he'd set up a drafting board until the snow came down so thick he couldn't help but notice it. Then he heard his phone ring. And the dogs bark. Maybe it was Holly. He jeans tightened below the belt. Ha. It was good to feel anything about a woman at all, but he felt more than lust for Holly. He'd love to see her. And the dogs could use some exercise before the six inches outside became a foot and a half. He could take a break. He had all his ideas on paper at least.

****

Bob didn't answer the phone. She hated when that happened. Then a text pinged. "Sorry missed yr call. Working this a.m. too. Will call after walk dogs!" Holly felt a rush of pleasure that was unlike anything except maybe drinking hot chocolate. Did she have supplies for this weather? She checked the pantry. Chocolate. Vanilla. Sugar. Bread. Pop tarts. Protein bars. Peanut butter. So far so good. She opened the fridge: Milk. Cheese. Butter. Apples. Jelly. Yogurt. Whipped cream in a can. Leftover chili from Uncle Eddie, even. She snagged an apple and shut the fridge door with a surge of energy. She was totally stocked up. She was making life on her own work. When her parents came in a few days, they'd be amazed to see her so self-sufficient. And happy. With a possible boyfriend.

The phone rang. She grabbed it. Bob! Finally!

They talked about nothing for an hour. Sharing work stories, sharing college stories. Her stomach growled. What with the phone call, then the visit from Sam, and then work, she had forgotten to eat. "I wish you could come over. I have leftover chili."

"That sounds good. I can come over."

"Well, but what about the snow?"

"I grew up here, Holly. Lake-effect storms are nothing new to me."

Wow. She felt all tingly thinking about her and Bob, snowed in. "But what about the dogs?"

135

"They'll be fine."

"But no, Luke said I'm going to be snowed in here at Blue Heaven until tomorrow morning."

"Oh. Well, I have a pickup truck. And a shovel."

"Or. Maybe you can bring the dogs?"

"Really? They haven't been invited anywhere yet."

"Well, consider them invited. I can heat us up some chili and put macaroni in it like my mom used to do."

"I think I have crackers here. But they might be stale."

"No, really. I just went shopping last week. I am all set. Really. I even have a couple of those beers I bought you a while ago."

"You do?"

She laughed. "Not a beer drinker here."

"Oh." He laughed too. "Well, I know you have chocolate, so that covers the all food groups."

"See you in a little while."

"Okay, see you soon."

She hung up the phone. This was a romance. A real romance. Or the start of one. She felt so comfortable with Bob. Like, even comfortable enough to tell him about her dilemma with the book contract and the condo. She just knew he'd understand.

Chapter Thirteen

Bob couldn't believe it. After they tore each other's clothes off and had sex twice, after they had a great lunch and he drank a beer, after sitting by the fire with the dogs at their feet, the snow coming down, darkness falling, the two of them snug together on the sofa, she had to go and spoil it.

"Say that again," Bob said.

Holly looked a little timid, as opposed to how she'd been with him all day.

Probably he had not misheard her. But he wanted to be sure.

"I was saying that the book contract—It's like the opportunity of a lifetime. And I have to move out of here in a couple of months, and I need more money than my job pays. I mean, the goal is a condo, but even to rent something, a house—I'd have to rent a room in someone's house on my salary, and I like having my own space—so the book deal just seems like the perfect solution. I just don't want you to be mad."

"What about Lily? Didn't she say she wouldn't cooperate? And didn't you promise your aunt and uncle that you would not write the book unless Lily gave her consent? And—and—didn't you tell me—what was that you said—yes, I know I heard you say you didn't sign the contract! You told me that, Holly!"

Bob felt like the whole thing with Holly had been a

cosmic joke. Just when he thought he was firing on all cylinders again, he stalled out.

"I did tell you that. It's the truth. I didn't sign the contract."

Bob was puzzled. Why would she bring it up, then?

"I mean, I still have an option to sign it. I can still consider it. I mean, if you, uh…"

"What does this have to do with me? This is about you, Holly. Your integrity. Your values. Your ethics." Bob felt really bad. He had liked her so much. But he hadn't known her. Not all of her. If he had to spell this all out to her, again—well, she obviously didn't get it. "What do *you* want to do?"

"I want to continue growing my career. I want to live an independent life. A good life. I want to be successful. A grown-up."

"But do you want to write this book?" He wasn't going to give up on her yet. He wanted to. It would be easier to leave, but that would be wrong after having sex with her. Twice in the last hour.

"I don't know."

She'd been so vocal before. Now her sentences were short, and she wasn't saying much. What? Did she want his permission? Was he supposed to prove he didn't care about Lily by saying sure, go ahead, write a book that will ruin somebody's life, maybe even your own cousin's life, if it helps you get your condo. If it makes you feel like a grown-up. He was seriously disgusted. With her, with himself. He didn't know.

"Well, I guess you have to think about it some more." Bob got up. The dogs stirred from their slumber. "I'm going to go."

"But wait. Bob. The snow."

"We're fine. We brought the shovel. Come on, guys." The dogs were already wagging their tails. At least someone in this house was happy. Holly looked like she might cry. He did not want to see that. He grabbed his coat from where he'd tossed it on the chair several hours and a lifetime ago.

"Bob! Are we okay?!"

"There is no 'we,' Holly."

Her face crunched up. He felt stupid.

"I thought there might be, but—shit." He ran his hand over his face.

"No. It's okay. I get it. I'm not moral enough for you. My ethics are not as black and white as they need to be for you. You don't want to figure things out with me. You don't want to help me sort out my life. Why should you? I hardly know you. Goodbye, Bob. It was fun. Until it wasn't."

When she finished her speech, she bolted down the hallway, slamming the bathroom door. He heard the toilet flush and the water running. He got the hell out of there. Why were women so complicated?

****

Holly turned on the sink faucets full blast. She flushed the toilet. She let the tears come. Well, they hadn't asked permission, they just did their thing. She blew her nose. Cried some more. She didn't think Bob had just been using her, and that this was a convenient excuse for him to break things off. She thought he liked her, but that he didn't like her enough. That made her cry harder. And to think she almost let herself love him.

She wasn't hungry, but she made herself hot chocolate, thinking if she could finish the hot drink without shedding any more tears, she would be doing good. That Bob! Honestly. Why she'd cry over him when he was clearly too high maintenance was beyond her. What was his problem, anyway? Well, could be that he was looking for reasons to reject her. Could be he was scarred by a former relationship. Could be he was too shallow to figure those things out. Also, could be he just didn't like who she was at her core. Well, too bad, because she liked who she was just fine.

Then the agent told her in a text that she was exercising her option to cancel the unsigned contract.

Holly didn't think about it before she texted back. "Why?"

"Story better told by seasoned professional."

From that text, Holly extrapolated that perhaps a staff writer from a scandal rag was looking for representation and story ideas plus a quick buck and had queried the agent who had taken Holly's idea and handed it over. All at once she was sick of the whole thing. Good riddance. She hadn't wanted to write that story anyway. It was too fraught. She couldn't hurt the people she cared about, which did not include Bob, she told herself. No, she was worried about Ruby and Uncle Eddie and Aunt Courtney.

An hour later, after writing out the latest developments in the Fun Divorce Club murder in her secret journal, what bothered her most about the agent's rejection were two words: seasoned professional. Holly was well on her way to becoming a seasoned professional. She was practically writing an entire town's newspaper by herself. And she was covering a murder!

Holly thought about the classified ads in the paper. She'd seen a few inquiries for rooms to rent. They just depressed her. The whole thing of finally giving up the ghost on her unrealistic dream of becoming a true-crime reporter was beyond depressing. Should she call Aunt Courtney? Or would she get over this and Bob's latest slap in the face, like, by the time her parents came to town? Or would Aunt Courtney try to be helpful and offer to introduce her to some people in the community with rooms to rent? The thought of that just buried her. She'd had her share of roommates in college, and she greatly preferred living alone. There had to be some little flat somewhere in town with a sloping roof and bad electricity that had her name on it.

A loud thump overhead brought her out of her sad ruminations. Her heart skidded to a stop, then started pumping overtime. What the hell? There it was again. She flew to the business end of the bungalow. An empty truck, or maybe it was an SUV, sat in the driveway. It was just a large dark lump in the dark, and she didn't want to turn on her light to find out because there was the thudding again. And a dragging sound. Like chains. Loud.

Then a woman's face appeared at the glass door, her mouth open in a silent scream. She banged on the door, her eyes pinned on Holly.

A really loud crash from the roof. Holly screamed.

The woman blinked, pounded on the door again. Holly wanted to tell her to be quiet because a murderer was on the roof, but the woman was shouting something Holly couldn't hear. Holly was not about to open her door to a strange terrified person standing at her door. She pulled her phone out of her jeans and dialed.

Chapter Fourteen

Holly listened. One ring. Two. She held up a finger signaling for the strange woman to wait. Finally Eva answered.

"Eva! There's a strange woman at my door and a truck in the driveway, and something scary is happening to the roof!"

"Holly?"

"Yes! What should I do?" But Holly was already unlocking the door. The woman did not have on gloves or a hat, and she looked about frozen.

"See who it is at the door. That's Luke on the roof. He keeps the snow off it, so the ceiling doesn't cave in with the weight."

"Oh," Holly said, letting the woman see she was actually talking to someone on the phone. "Who are you?" she said to the lady in a fluffy black parka.

"Phoebe," the frozen woman said, stepping inside.

Holly had not recognized her with all the snow covering her hair. Which was tucked into a cap. And she didn't have makeup on. And her coat was puffy, making her look like some kind of snow monster.

"It's Phoebe, Eva," Holly said. "Sorry to bother you."

"Okay, sorry I didn't warn you about the roof. Guess they don't shovel roofs downstate?"

"Not that I know of." Holly said goodbye to Eva

and watched Phoebe's snow melt all over the floor. "Ah, what can I do for you, Phoebe?"

Phoebe! Possible murderess melting snow all over the floor. How on earth did she get here? And where were her children?

"I live next door to Luke's mom. He always plows our street, so I asked him if I could catch a ride out to Blue Heaven. I need to talk to you."

"Uh, okay." Holly had a feeling she knew where this was going.

"I am not a murderer, so I wish you'd quit implying that all over town!"

"I didn't imply that. And certainly not all over town. I've been conducting interviews for the paper. Just gathering facts."

"Well, your facts look like accusations to me. You better not print that stuff you said to my ex. I mean it."

Phoebe was a petite woman, not much taller than Holly, if a bit rounder. She was a spitfire. Holly could totally see her sending smut videos to her lover of the moment. Another crash overhead. Holly was getting used to it, now that she knew it was Luke.

"Now see, right there. That sounds like a threat. If I thought you were a murderer, saying stuff like that would lend credence to the theory."

"What? I'm just saying…" Phoebe started to shiver. Her motorcycle boots had been less than adequate in this snow. "Just—leave me alone. I have kids. Moms are not murderers!"

Luke came down from a ladder Holly in her terror had not noticed before. He disappeared around where the shed was, toting the ladder.

"Looks like Luke is done," Holly said. She hoped

Phoebe wasn't expecting an invitation to tea.

"Well. Okay, but do you believe me?"

Holly hadn't known what to believe, but just the little crack of Phoebe's voice right then made her think she didn't do it.

"Of course I believe you. You are clearly not a murderer. Not that I ever thought you were! I just have to keep an open mind. It's my job." Holly was totally placating this madwoman, but it was good insurance. If Phoebe was a murderer, at least she wouldn't come after the town reporter who professed to believe she was innocent.

"Well, okay then. I'm glad I came over. It's been horrible since Jordan died. Even before that, with the whole video thing. I can't believe I made that video for him. I'm such an idiot. It was a stupid impulse, and it ruined my life!"

"Then why were you getting back together with him?"

"I wasn't! I was just trying to make him think I was interested—I don't know. I wanted him to delete the video. I figured I could make him do it if I tried hard enough. You know."

Holly knew. They should really call their group the Sexy Divorce Club.

"When I made it, I never thought he'd show it to anyone. Obviously. Was I wrong. He couldn't wait to show it to all his friends. He broke up with me, like, two days after I sent it."

"Men suck."

"Yeah, well, Bob Bryman was not the brightest idea. He's been in love with Lily forever. Since they were kids, practically."

Holly shouldn't be surprised everyone knew about her and Bob. But could the news of their latest split really be all over town? In the middle of a snowstorm?

"Why? What have you heard about Bob and me?"

"It's a small town. Everybody hears everything. Well, almost."

Luke picked up the shovel and cleared the side porch. He went around the house, probably doing the front lake-view porch.

Phoebe snapped up her puffy coat. "No, just...well, I did hear you two left the Sleigh Bell Ball together. And from what you're saying now I take it things didn't go so well?"

Holly shrugged. "Win some, lose some."

"This is not a great town to meet men in. I'm just saying."

"I don't know." Holly thought about Sam and Bob. Maybe not perfect mates for life, but two good-looking guys in one month was pretty decent, even down state.

Luke's truck roared to life, and he beeped the horn.

"Nice talking to you, Holly. Just remember. I did not do it. I'm the victim here, too." And Phoebe left. Holly waved at Luke and closed the door. She locked it and then went into her quarters and locked that door too. She really wished she had a cupcake. Her life just kept sucking worse.

****

Things did not lighten up at work the next morning. Colette piled the work on, which was kind of her, because while it did little to dissipate her gloom, it helped Holly forget about Bob. And the agent. And her brush with a would-be murderess. She actually felt sorry for Phoebe. Even if she had murdered Jordan, her reasons were pretty solid.

Late that night, Holly added to her notes in her secret notebook. She was less sure of herself than ever. If Phoebe was still a suspect, and Will was once again a suspect, then why wouldn't Kelly also be a suspect? Holly had sympathy for all of them, couldn't picture any of them as a murderer. But someone had to have done it. Someone was fooling her. Maybe it was time to scratch the surface of Kelly's life, or even Patrick's life, or Quinn's life, or for that matter, India's life, and she'd probably get dirt under her nails. Everybody had something to hide, and when you were divorced with kids, there was just that much more to cover up and try to forget.

Hell, she might even have to put Colette on the suspect list. But no. Not Colette. She had to have somebody to believe in. Some tenuous thing to trust. Otherwise, when her folks got into town tomorrow, they'd sniff out her gloom. They'd sense she was depressed. They'd offer to pay for some sessions with Aunt Courtney.

They might even get out of her the whole failed plan about the true-crime book and the condo. Then they'd offer to put a down payment on a condo for her. Of course they would. And she couldn't let them. They needed to save for their retirement. They'd already spent a fortune on her college education. She had to prove to them she was worth it. That she could make a life on her own. Even if it was a sucky life.

And now she needed a new secret notebook, too, because she'd filled this one, both sides, with her inky scribble, disjoined thoughts, and half-assed theories about the Fun Divorce Club killer.

Chapter Fifteen

Holly's parents arrived in Blue Lake two days before Christmas and one day before Holly's birthday.

"I need to leave a little early today," Holly said to Colette. It had been an uneventful day at the paper. There was no news on the murder case, and the condo story had been played out for now. The paper was filled with Christmas letters from Blue Lake residents and a lot of small puff pieces on local businesses and their special hours on Christmas Eve. Then on Christmas Day, the whole town shut down, including the paper. Actually, the paper would close on Christmas Eve, too. So it wasn't like Colette didn't know Holly was leaving early.

"Fine! Have a great Christmas! Say hi to your family." Colette was a hugger. Holly was not, not a huge hugger. But she accepted Colette's embrace with as much good grace as she could, considering she was still battered and bruised after her breakups with Bob and the agent. After her shattered dream of the condo. Not to mention thinking for a minute that a murderer was knocking on her door and that she might be the next victim.

When Holly got to the bungalow, she'd talked herself into putting on a happy face for her mom and dad. It seemed to work. Her dad brought in the suitcases, gave Holly a kiss, and headed out to his brother's bar. Her mom unpacked and made a big fuss over the bungalow. "You have such a nice place here, and right on the water, too!" Holly didn't bother to tell her mom that it was only her place until tourist season. She didn't want to think about it.

Her mom handed her a big heavy box. "A housewarming present," she said.

"Mom, you didn't have to!" Her parents always showered her with gifts this time of year. Her birthday was a big deal, with cake and ice cream and usually a party, but of course not this year, even though it was on Christmas Eve. And then they did another celebration on Christmas for the holiday. This Christmas Aunt Courtney was having the dinner at her house.

Holly ripped open the present from her mom, thinking out of nowhere that if the dogs were here, she wouldn't be able to leave the wrapping paper on the floor for a second or they'd try to eat it. She kept her eyes lowered on the box so her mom, an expert thought-reader, could not see her stupid sad eyes. She was determined not to think about Bob.

She lifted the lid off the box. Inside, her mom had arranged two cookbooks, an apron, several cookie sheets, a large bar of baker's chocolate, and a red standing mixer.

"Wow! Thank you!" Holly had no idea how to use the mixer or what she was supposed to use it for, but it was pretty. It would look nice in her new hovel, wherever that might be.

The apron said "Cooked by an Angel," and it made Holly think about the angel on top of her tree from Bob. Oh, Bob, she needed to get him off her mind.

Her mom started unpacking the grocery bags her

dad had brought in earlier. Flour, nuts, baking powder, and baking soda, plus a whole bunch of other stuff Holly wasn't sure how to use. She must have looked puzzled because her mom said, "Cheer up, dear. We're baking cookies to take to Aunt Courtney! Five different kinds! All your favorites! Chocolate always makes you smile."

Holly smiled on cue, then put on the apron.

The cookie baking took most of the evening, so it was good that Dad brought home fish and chips for dinner from Uncle Eddie's bar.

Chapter Sixteen

Holly had no idea acting happy could be so exhausting. She took a hot shower, trying to recover after dinner with Mom and Dad and that unwelcome guest, their curiosity. They could not know how sad she was. They could not know she felt like a failure as a grown-up. Well, not a complete failure. Just a bit of one. Acting happy was a real challenge. Maybe she'd go to bed early with a book. Mom was planning a little brunch tomorrow, just family, but that would be one more hurdle.

For the first time she could remember, Holly was not excited about her birthday. Not excited for Christmas to come. She was actually looking forward to being back at work. She got out of the shower and forced herself to put on jeans, when really she'd like to cuddle up in front of the television in her jammies and watch reruns of *Castle*.

Instead, she watched some sort of PBS program with her parents. Then she made the "really good book/exhausted" excuse she'd mentally prepared.

Her mom wasn't buying it. "Dear, what's wrong? You can tell us."

"We both know something's up," her dad said. Ganging up on her. She'd forgotten how they did that. It wore her down. She searched her brain for something to tell them. Something that wouldn't be too excruciating to disclose.

"Didn't Uncle Eddie tell you? About the true-crime book?"

"He didn't mention a thing," her dad said.

"Well, dear, is this the book idea that an agent was interested in?"

"Yes, Mom." Holly thought how best to put the weight of her break-up with Bob and the whole ruined dream of a new condo into the agent story. "I didn't want you to worry. It's nothing really."

"Tell us. What happened?"

"Well, I had this idea…" Holly explained about the true-crime book deal gone wrong. "So, it's for the best, I know, but it's just, um, you know, a slight setback." She hoped that would be good enough to hold back any more loving but annoying questioning from her parents.

"You did the right thing, Holly." Her dad didn't know that actually she had not done anything. The agent had.

"What you're working on now for the paper—that Fun Divorce Club death thing—you're doing such a good job reporting those stories. I feel like I'm watching a movie when I read your updates. And that interview with the guy accused of murder! I was a little frightened for you, dear, going to his home like that."

"Oh, it was nothing. I knew he was innocent."

"We were quite concerned. But Uncle Eddie said the police had not ruled out accidental poisoning, and you didn't say anything different in your stories, so we forced ourselves not to rush up here to your rescue."

Holly smiled at that. They didn't know the half of it. And if she could help it, they never would. She basked a little in her mom's praise. Then something clicked. Duh. Took her long enough.

"Mom. You gave me an idea. I can pitch this story to the agent. Even though it's still unfolding. And probably it is going to turn out to be an accident, but I could make it suspenseful." Holly knew that the poisoning had not been an accident. Once the story unfolded, once the murderer was caught, she'd have her ending. But she didn't want her parents, or anyone in town, to worry. People were a little wary, a little more on guard, but with the possibility of an accidental poisoning, nobody's Christmas was going to be totally ruined. Except Will's. "And maybe I could change the ending. Sell it as crime fiction. Like a thriller." Holly actually thought this would be a good idea, if she had any interest in writing fiction. Which she didn't. She liked facts.

****

Bob was immersed in work when the phone rang on Christmas Eve. He hoped it wasn't his brother again, urging him to attend the brunch for Holly. He almost ignored the phone but then picked it up when he saw who it was. Not his brother.

"Hey, Marianne." He knew what was coming. He didn't want to deal with it, but he would. He listened to her for a minute and then said, "I'll be there in ten minutes. Thanks."

Downtown was crammed with cars. It could have been tourist season, but actually it was just the day before Christmas when the men in town rushed to get their shopping done. Every store was open. Everyone had a sale. He had to wait in line in the jewelry store, which gave him plenty of time to think about what an idiot he'd been. What had he been thinking, special ordering that necklace for Holly? It was too expensive, for one thing. She was worth it, of course, but it might send the wrong message. Also, they were over. But he missed her. He didn't like admitting that.

"Bob? What do you think?"

Marianne was behind the glass cases. She had a black velvet cloth out, and on it she had arranged the thin rose-gold chain with the tiny typewriter charm.

"Nice," he said. It was so Holly. He should just give it to her. He certainly couldn't return it. "Will you gift wrap it?" He could go to the brunch. Give her the necklace. That way it wouldn't sit on his mantel or in a drawer somewhere. He didn't know any other writers. Well, Rachel, but she'd retired. And the necklace was not her style. Although she was probably old enough to have worked with an actual typewriter in her day.

While a sales assistant, at her own little spot by the door, wrapped the gift, Bob paid for it with his credit card. For him, buying something like a gold necklace was not going to break the bank. He'd never had a moment in his life when he worried about money. He came from wealth; that was never an issue. But what about Holly? She was trying so hard to make it on her own. And that was all the book thing had been about. Trying to do what she loved and also feed, house, and clothe herself. Also, she'd really been asking him, he realized now as he signed his credit card receipt. She'd wanted his opinion about what she should do. She wanted to discuss it with him, give him her side of the story. Talk it over, like friends or lovers would do.

"Hope the lucky girl enjoys it," Marianne said.

"Me too," Bob said. He went over to the gift wrap station, waiting for the bow on the festively papered box to be tied. As the young clerk carefully stowed his purchase in a tiny shopping bag, Bob had the passing thought that he had not tried for a minute to see things from Holly's point of view. Yet obviously, she'd tried to see things from his side. She'd even asked him what he thought she should do. Why did he have to get all angry at her, twice? Love shy after Lily, he guessed. But Holly was not Lily. Not even close.

He took the gift, hoping it would be enough to make her forgive him. What kind of a jerk has amazing sex with a woman and then dumps her right before Christmas? If she refused to forgive him, he wouldn't blame her. He'd been putting her down and picking her up from the minute she got to town. She probably should be wary. On the other hand, she'd invited him to her brunch. That had to mean something.

He left the store in a completely different frame of mind from when he'd entered. He was glad he'd bought Holly the necklace. He wanted to give it to her. He wanted to make her smile again.

Chapter Seventeen

Bob. Holly couldn't believe it. How did he have the nerve to show up at her birthday party after the way they'd left things? But there were two dozen people in her house, and her mom was so excited, and Bob's brother was here, and well, her mom had probably invited Bob.

Holly stood next to the tree. She couldn't move if she had wanted to. Bob was here and so was Sam, and she couldn't miss the measured look they gave each other. But then Sam went over to Phoebe, and Phoebe took a step back. The look on her face was not happy. What the heck was Sam saying to Phoebe?

Amanda pinched Holly's arm. "Are you still seeing Bob? You didn't tell me!"

"No, oh, well, we're kind of off and on, if you know what I mean. Hey, did Sam ever date Phoebe?"

"Honey, you know those people in the Fun Divorce Club! They all date each other. I can't keep track. But well, yes, I seem to recall seeing them around town together once or twice."

Sam? In the Fun Divorce Club?

"I didn't know Sam was divorced." He hadn't been at the party the night Jordan died. Colette would have said.

"Well, he is. He doesn't like to talk about it."

Bob was coming toward them. He was holding a

tiny little box with the cutest little bow. For her?

"I'll leave and let you two talk."

"No! Stay with me, Amanda. Honestly, I can't believe all these Fun Divorce Club people showed up, and I didn't know Sam was divorced, and I need to know, when exactly did he date Phoebe?"

"You'll be fine, Holly. We can talk later, but Bob looks like he wants to say something to you now, so I'm going to grab another one of those jam thumbprints you made. You are a great cook."

Before Holly could say "I'm not," Bob was at her side. His eyes slid into hers, and he handed her the gift. "Happy birthday, Holly."

She reached out and took the little box. Her voice had gone somewhere. She nodded. She knew she needed to say something to him, but had no idea what it would be.

"You must be Bob," her mom said. "Thanks for coming." Her mom was saying some more things, but Holly didn't hear her. She couldn't talk. She couldn't hear. Damn, it made her mad. Bob had a lot of nerve, coming here. Well, yeah, he really did. It was nice...maybe? She wasn't sure. He made her feel so off balance. But he was here, and so was everyone else in Blue Lake she'd ever spoken to, even once, so she'd make the best of it and be gracious like her mother taught her. If she could coax her voice back from wherever it had gone.

"Thank you for coming, everyone," her dad said. Holly realized they'd been waiting for Bob. Now it was time to eat. But first he'd give his little speech about how beloved Holly was and what a treasure she was and the other embarrassing stuff he said every year.

Holly held her breath. This was the most difficult part of the day. The rest would all be fine. Even with Bob here.

"I'm an idiot," Bob whispered.

She heard that but didn't reply. What was she supposed to say? *I know* didn't quite cover it.

"What's he done now?" Sam appeared at her side from the other end of the room, so she was sandwiched between the two men she'd dated since coming to town. Damn. Awkward didn't begin to cover it. "Why are you an idiot, Bob? I mean, I agree, but specifically, what did you do to Holly? Because if you've hurt her, I have a problem with that."

Holly wished she could fall through the floor and into her own bed, where she could hide under the covers until this party was over. Instead, she had to take the glass of champagne the Two Sisters were handing out, because her dad was about to toast to the best Christmas present he and her mother had ever received. It happened every year. The sisters started passing out glasses of champagne for the adults, juice for the kids.

She pulled Sam off to a corner and left Bob standing there without a word. "Why didn't you tell me you were divorced?!" she whispered.

Sam shrugged it off. No big deal. "Everybody is, well, almost."

"You could have told me!"

"If we'd had more than one date, maybe I would have. It just didn't seem that important."

"But you were in the Fun Divorce Club. Where were you the night of the party? The night Jordan was poisoned? Why weren't you there? Was it because Phoebe and Jordan were getting back together again?

Were you jealous?"

"Whoa, whoa," Sam said. "It's not what you think. I don't know what you've heard, but I was not one of those Fun Divorce Club people like the rest of them. Yes, I went for a while when I was new in town. It wasn't my thing. End of story."

Champagne glasses were thrust into their hands, and Holly's dad started the toast. Holly had to be quiet and she tried to listen, but her heart was hammering and her mind was racing. She should not have confronted Sam. What if he was the one who had killed Jordan? What would he do? Leave town in the middle of her party? Get away with it? Or worse, stay and do something even more horrible than poisoning Jordan?

Every glass in the room was raised, and every person drank. Even Holly. He wouldn't poison a room full of people, would he? Sam offered his arm. She took it, trying hard not to let her thoughts show on her face. She was being stupid. Paranoid. Wasn't she?

She sat at the head of the table, her mom and dad on either side of her. The sisters served the meats, roast beef and ham. Her guests passed bowls of mashed potatoes and rolls and Holly's favorite roasted Brussels-sprout casserole. There was gravy and cranberry sauce and salad and pears with blue cheese crumbled on top of them. A broccoli slaw. Shrimp. Spicy sausages. Baked beans. There was enough food to serve a football team.

Holly looked down the long table to all the faces she'd come to know this past month. Even Phoebe smiled at her. At the far end of the table, three teenaged girls, including her cousin Ruby, texted and giggled. Her uncle Eddie did not tell them to put away their phones. And when the littlest guest, who was either Colette's or Phoebe's baby, refused to try a Brussels sprout, nobody paid attention. Bob was next to her mother, and Sam was further down the table next to Phoebe. Phoebe wasn't looking grim. In fact, she was smiling at something Sam said, so that was good.

Holly didn't taste a bite of her meal. She was sure all the food was delicious, but it was lost on her. She took tiny bites and mentally prepared her thank-you speech, traditionally given after the meal but before she opened her gifts. What was in the little box Bob had given her? And more importantly, was Sam a murderer? But he hadn't been there that night. Not until after she'd gotten there. It wasn't possible. Her head hurt. She blamed the champagne.

Finally, her mom gave her the sign. Time to thank her guests.

"Once or twice when I was younger, my parents surprised me with a special party on my birthday. But usually I knew it would just be close family and friends." She had to act as normal as possible and then talk to Colette. Maybe she'd forgotten Sam had been there? "This year, I'm so thankful for the surprise of all of you." That's all she could say because she had to find a tissue as her eyes were tearing up. She was a little afraid, a little angry, a little overcome. Her mom pressed a tissue into her hand. Holly leaned over and kissed her mom and said thank you, and then she did the same to her dad.

"Time to open my presents yet?" She'd ask Colette to help her. Say something to her while Sam was still occupied with Phoebe. She stole a glance at them. Sam's smile could break his face. He was making every effort to be charming, but Phoebe wasn't smiling anymore. She kept glancing around, like she wanted someone to rescue her.

Everyone laughed at her comment about opening presents.

"We have gifts for the children first," her dad said.

Of course they did. Her parents thought of everything. She kept one eye on Sam, trying to be discreet. He couldn't know what kind of crazy thoughts were swirling through her brain right now.

The sisters were clearing, and coffee was being set up next to the pies and cookies and a coconut cake that Holly knew she'd never be able to taste.

While the little kids screamed with delight and headed for the tree bursting with wrapped gifts, the bigger girls acted casual and went over to a sofa, still close enough to the tree to snag a present. Holly thought about how Jordan had flirted with India's daughter. India had as good a reason to kill Jordan as Sam did. And she had means and opportunity, which Sam did not. Even Phoebe had a better reason than Sam to want Jordan dead. She was being silly. Still, it couldn't hurt to ask Colette about Sam.

Holly's dad put on his silly Santa hat—she couldn't believe he'd brought it—and passed out presents. Her mom went over to help. The grown-ups served themselves coffee or poured more wine. Most of them allowed themselves to be talked into getting on coats and boots and accompanying the children outside. Before she could go out with the kids, Holly grabbed Colette's glass and led her over to the drinks table.

"I need to talk to you," Holly said.

"What?" Colette absently sipped the wine Holly

had poured her. "Aren't you having another?"

"I have a headache. Listen." Holly looked over Colette's shoulder. Most everyone was gone. Phoebe was walking away from Sam, toward Colette and Holly. Sam turned and went downstairs. To play with the kids? Not likely. He was probably leaving. Laughter and shouting rose from outside. That was good. "Was Sam at the party the night Jordan died?"

"No, why?"

"Sure, he was," Phoebe said, entering the circle of two. Then Amanda joined them. "He stopped by for a minute—I don't know—maybe before you got there? He said he had to work. But he gave Will a bottle of scotch. He had a drink, too, I think."

Amanda was shaking her head. "Sam wasn't on duty that night. He was called in after the 911 came through."

"Now that I think of it—a car did pull out of Will's drive just as I was parking. I remember thinking maybe the party was a dud before it even started. Then I forgot about it." Colette looked puzzled. "Why?"

Holly was thinking furiously. Mistletoe grew in Kentucky just across the border where Sam was from in southern Ohio. And hadn't he just come back from there right before their date? And didn't he have the means to plant evidence at Will's? But why? What was his motive?

"Sam was like the favorite new guy for a while there," Phoebe told Holly. "Are you going to be okay? You look funny."

Holly nodded. Her mind was furiously spinning a new thread to this complicated piece of work.

"I need to go outside with the kids," Phoebe said.

"No, wait," Holly said. She gave Phoebe a weak smile. "You dated Sam, right?"

Phoebe made a face. "For a minute. He was too intense."

"What do you mean?"

Amanda was uncharacteristically silent. She wanted to know, too.

"Well..." Phoebe lowered her voice even though the four of them were the last people besides the sisters, who were cleaning up, in the room. "Maybe it was because Jordan and I had just broken up. I was in love with Jordan. We had a fight—well, you know what about."

Amanda didn't interrupt, and neither did Colette, so obviously Phoebe wasn't surprised or upset that the video story had gotten around, at least to them.

"Anyway, I went out with Sam to make Jordan jealous. I didn't pay too much attention at the time, but Sam was awfully sweet on me awfully fast. And he was jealous of Jordan. I admit I was mostly still focused on Jordan, so any man would probably be hurt by that. I guess I was obvious. But, I mean, when I told him I was getting back with Jordan, Sam asked me to marry him. He said Jordan never would propose. He said he'd never loved anybody the way he loved me and Jordan was a jerk. He told me Jordan had shown him the private video I'd made for Jordan." Phoebe shot a shamed look at Amanda, who seemed to be all nonjudgmental ears.

"Okay," Holly said, thinking, *bingo, motive.* "Then you got back with Jordan..." She hoped Phoebe had more to the story.

"After just a couple of dates with Sam, who was

annoying me with his possessiveness anyway, Jordan wanted me back. And despite what he'd done with my video, I decided to give him another chance. Maybe I wanted to convince him to give me the video or delete it or something. Anyway, Sam was really mad. He said we were soul mates."

"When was that?"

"Well, it had to be October. We had a Halloween party, the club, and Sam never showed. I just thought, you know, get over yourself. But I was glad, too. Then when Sam stopped by at the Thanksgiving weekend party, I thought, okay, good, he got over it. He barely said hi to me that night."

"I...I wonder if Sam was upset enough to kill Jordan?"

"Holly, a few days ago you thought I killed Jordan!"

"Right, but I didn't really. I just had to find out. I had to talk to you. The police didn't seem to be doing anything." Holly looked at Amanda and Phoebe. "That's why! He wanted to frame Will. Sam didn't want any other suspects. No wonder he warned me off you, Phoebe."

"Where is Sam?"

"Good question. Amanda, what do you think? Could Sam have done it? Should you call the chief?" Holly didn't wait around for Amanda's answer. She rushed toward the stairs, looking for Ruby, looking for Sam.

Chapter Eighteen

"Ruby!"

Holly crossed the room and ran down the stairs. Where was Sam? Earlier he had gone on and on about how he couldn't wait for her to open her gift. Now he disappears? Without saying goodbye?

Holly prayed Amanda was already on her cell phone with the chief.

A shout from her quarters. Ruby! Holly could hear the giggles of the young girls in her living room. Good. Maybe Sam was not with them. But what if he got away? She rushed in to make sure the girls were okay, and there they were, the three of them, with Sam sitting in the middle of their circle, grinning.

"Oh, hi, Holly," Sam said. "I really like your cousin."

Holly might not be a cop, but in that frozen moment, Sam smelled evil to her. Did he really not know she'd figured him out? How stupid did he think she was, anyway?

Ruby blushed. Clearly, she didn't know what an evil murderer she was flirting with. And Heather was just as bad, batting her fake eyelashes. Really, did Colette let Heather wear those? Was this a thing now for kids? The other girl, India's daughter, Whitney, didn't seem quite so keen on Sam as the other two. She made a subtle face of distress behind Sam's back toward Holly. Okay, Holly bet that had to do with the way Jordan had hit on her. She didn't trust men of a certain age. At this point, neither did Holly.

"Sam, can I talk to you?" Holly said. She didn't know what she was going to talk to him about. She just hoped that the chief would get here soon and arrest him. And she wanted to get him away from the girls.

"Don't go, Sam," Heather said. "You're funny."

"Haha," said Whitney. She poked Heather hard in the arm.

"Ouch," Heather said.

Sam just sat there in Holly's living room, looking smug. "What's the matter, Holly? Jealous?"

"What? No! I just need to ask you something."

"Ask away. I have no secrets from these girls. We're all friends, here, right?"

"Sam, stop it. Girls, get upstairs. Now."

Ruby looked at her like she'd grown an extra head, but she got up to do as Holly demanded. Heather and Whitney skipped away, Whitney giving Holly an air kiss and a grateful smile. Heather's look was not as nice. God, if those girls only knew who Sam really was. Meanwhile, Sam had grabbed Ruby's hand in an attempt at being playful. Holly marched over and smacked his hand off her cousin's.

"I need to talk to Sam alone for a minute," Holly said. When Ruby finally left the room, Holly noticed the snowball fight outside. Grown-ups and children alike were shrieking and throwing snow, falling down and getting up to do it all over again. Good. Everyone was occupied.

"Think you're pretty smart, don't you?" Sam said.

"What? No. Not smart enough, actually."

"Think you got me all figured out," he said.

"Finally. Took me long enough."

"Well, birthday girl, why don't you open your present?"

"What? It's upstairs. That's not what this is about."

Sam stood up and grabbed her by both arms. "Oh no? Then what? Trying to make Bob jealous?" Sam shook her, hard. He let go of her with one hand, but only so he could smack her across the face.

"Oww!" She didn't know what she'd been expecting, confronting a murderer, but it hadn't been physical violence. Maybe a denial. But no. Sam's flat eyes, the color of an angry lake, made her shudder. "What's wrong with you?" How did Sam know she knew he had murdered Jordan? Had he heard them? Had he been lurking on the stairs until he heard her call out to Ruby?

"You think I killed Jordan. But you don't have any proof. Plus, it's pretty stupid of you to be here with me alone, don't you think?"

"We are not alone," Holly said, nodding toward the porch where her dad, Bob, Ernie, Daniel, and Uncle Eddie stood. They stood in a line while her dad tried to open the door. He was yelling something at her or at Sam. The door was locked, and Sam grabbed her arm, not letting her open it. She saw Bob slip from the line. Maybe he was coming to get her. She hoped so. Meanwhile, she had to save herself. "Get your hands off me," she said.

Sam reached into his jacket and pulled out a gun, pointing it at her chest. Her father got quiet.

She couldn't take her eyes off Sam's weapon. "Sam. Stop it. Why are you doing this?" She thought fast. She'd been making up arguments for and against everybody in the Fun Divorce Club. Why couldn't she come up with something for Sam? Then, despite her heart slamming her chest like a hammer, she did. "If you really killed Jordan, you'd be halfway out of the state by now. But you're here. So of course you didn't do it."

She really didn't know why Sam had stuck around, but he was cornered. He knew it, and like a frenzied animal, he was protecting himself the only way he knew how. What a psycho. She was more sure than ever that he'd killed Jordan. And she would lie through her teeth about it if it would make him put his gun down.

"Shut up, you stupid bitch. I came here to give Phoebe a taste of her own medicine. She used me to make Jordan jealous, so I was using you the same way. Why do you think I acted jealous of Bob and made a big deal about a stupid little present every time she came around us? Don't get all excited. It's drugstore cologne. But see, it's working, she's into me again."

Psycho and delusional.

"Yeah, but you'd better put the gun away. She won't like that."

Sam put his gun back in his holster. "That's it?" He laughed. "Most chicks like the Glock. Maybe not pointed at them, but they like handling it. Phoebe even asked me to take her out shooting."

His laugh chilled her. She felt frozen in place. Where was the chief? Where was everyone? Her eyes flicked to the windows, and although the men, minus Bob, still stood there on guard, no children were in sight. No women, either.

"Ah, okay, well, maybe I got a little hot-headed there with the gun. No harm, no foul, am I right?"

"Sure, right."

"Sam!" It was Phoebe. "Hey, can we talk?" Phoebe's figure flitted across the archway leading to the kitchen. Sam, sick in so many ways, including being a lovesick fool, actually smiled. Every tense bone in his body relaxed.

Holly was a short woman, and Sam was a tall man. This worked in her favor. She elbowed him hard in the privates, and caught off guard, he doubled over screaming. She ran to the door where her father and Daniel and her uncle Eddie stood and quickly flicked open the lock. The men rushed in. Daniel and Uncle Eddie held Sam's arms, while her dad grabbed the gun from Sam's holster. Before she knew he was in the room, Bob was there, holding her.

"Chief's here," he whispered.

The chief came in and cuffed Sam.

"Hey, what's this about?" Sam said. "Just a misunderstanding between friends, right, Holly?"

Holly just shook her head. The chief was reading Sam his rights. Now the chief would look for evidence where it had probably been all along. In Sam's house.

Two hours later, everyone had been questioned, given statements and had gone home except Bob. Her mom and dad didn't want Holly out of their sight, but Bob promised they'd just be upstairs by the tree.

He held her hand and led her over to a sofa. "I have so much to say to you," he said. "But first, just open this."

Holly had forgotten it was her birthday, forgotten her presents. All she could think about was that the Fun

Divorce Club killer had been caught. And the town was safe. It would be a merry Christmas in Blue Lake after all. Holly was shaken but not as badly as Ruby and Heather when they realized they'd been flirting with a murderer. Aunt Courtney had hugged Holly and called her the bravest girl.

Holly, slightly dazed, tugged at the pretty ribbon on the little package. She opened the gift and stared down at the rose-gold typewriter on its delicate chain. She burst into tears. "Oh, Bob," she said. "I love it." She carefully extricated the chain from the jewel box and held it up to her neck. "Will you fasten it for me? I'm never taking it off."

Bob hooked her clasp and kissed her neck. They held each other like that for a long time. Finally Bob said, not letting her go, "Holly if you take me back, I promise I will not break things off again. I'm an idiot. I can't explain; I just wasn't ready for this. You surprised me. But I figured it out. I want to be with you. I care about you. I might love you. Will you give me another chance?"

Holly nodded. She hoped her kiss said the rest.

Chapter Nineteen

Christmas morning dawned cold and clear in Blue Lake. Rachel woke up before her grandchildren, happy and content to be home with them. It was like getting a second chance to savor the kind of happiness and innocence only children bring to Christmas. She checked the clock, then put on her velour tracksuit with the embroidered Santa cap on it. She needed to go eat those cookies and drink that milk before the kids woke up. She quietly crept down the stairs with alacrity. Then she sat with a cup of coffee and practiced looking surprised for when she unwrapped Ernie's gift. She'd been very clear which ring she wanted when he casually asked her which one she liked best in the jewelry store's catalog.

****

Ernie opened his eyes to another day alive and counted himself lucky. He'd done something really foolish or really smart—he wasn't sure. He still hadn't decided after he'd had a cup of coffee and a piece of pie Rachel had made a few days ago. He looked to the front door where shopping bags filled with wrapped gifts, and one special present for Rachel, waited for him to get ready and go to Rachel's house. Now that she was back home, she'd invited him over to watch the children open their presents from Santa. Christmas might be all about kids, but Ernie felt a bit like a big kid himself. He couldn't wait to see the look in Rachel's eyes when she opened her gift.

****

Colette woke up when Jenny snuggled into bed with her. "Mommy, it's Christmas!" Jenny said. "Wake up!"

"What time is it?" It felt like two a.m.

Leroy piped up. "Six o'clock already!"

Colette had to admit, that was a little later than usual for her kids. "Okay, well, can I brush my teeth?"

"Can we go downstairs? Ernie's here, he just ringed the doorbell. And Granny is down there. She said hi to him. And it smells like bacon, too," Jenny said. Heather snorted but without rancor from her position at the doorway.

"Wait for me, please. I'll just be a minute." Colette herded the kids into the hall with their big sister, closed the door, and threw on some yoga pants. She opened the door. "Does everyone have their slippers on? I didn't think so."

Jenny whooped with joy. Leroy and Heather just ignored her. Colette thought fleetingly about her ex. The kids hadn't mentioned him, and she wouldn't either. She was very glad to be here. She looked out the bedroom window. It had started to snow.

****

Bob woke up next to Holly. Not in her bedroom. That probably would not go over with the folks. But they'd sat up all night talking in front of the fire. He wrapped his arms around her and kissed her neck. She smelled so good, like cookies. He thought about last night, how she'd been so sweet and giving. She'd told him about signing the alternate book deal and had worried because of Ruby's small part in yesterday's debacle. She wondered what to do about some part Phoebe had played in the unfolding of the case, because she didn't want Phoebe or her kids to be hurt by her words. Bob had told her he knew she'd find the right words.

She stirred in his arms, and her hand came up to his hair. She ran her fingers through his messy hair, making it worse.

"Good morning, gorgeous," he said.

"Morning!" Holly bolted upright. "Oh my God, it's Christmas!"

"It is," Bob agreed.

"Merry Christmas," she said, kissing him.

That took a while. Luckily her parents appeared to be heavy sleepers.

"I love you, Holly," Bob said. "I know it's crazy and fast, but really I think I started to love you the first time I saw you at the library. You pulled me up out of a dark hole. It all started then. I just didn't know it. I thought it was the dogs or the condo project, but it was you all along."

"The dogs!" Holly said. "Don't you need to feed them?"

Bob felt like a very bad father. He needed to get home.

"It's okay," Holly said. "I have to write that piece for the *Tribune* anyway."

Not many people would prefer to write a story all day Christmas Day, but Holly would.

****

Fun Divorce Club Killer Caught
At a brunch in her honor on Christmas Eve, this

reporter learned firsthand that Officer Sam Carpenter, a person known to all in Blue Lake as local law enforcement, murdered Fun Divorce Club member Jordan Stanica in cold blood on November 27 during a holiday party. Carpenter, it has been revealed, used a paper lunch bag to transport a poisonous variety of mistletoe purchased on a visit to his hometown in Kenosha, Kentucky, one week previous to the murder. Carpenter then emptied the remains of the mistletoe from the bag into the trash of the homeowner who hosted the party, William Hudson. Hudson was briefly detained and released by police. The bag containing the lethal mistletoe was recovered from Carpenter's home where he'd discarded it in his recycle bin. Police chief Harlan Tucker recovered this crucial evidence after arresting Carpenter, who remains in county jail under lock and key.

A word from the author...

Along with a twenty-year career as an English teacher, I have been a staff reviewer for *Romantic Times* and *Publishers Weekly* and written features for popular magazines, including *Woman's World. BLUE LAKE CHRISTMAS MYSTERY* is my fifth novel for The Wild Rose Press. I live in metro Detroit with my husband, Al. We have two grown sons. Since 2002, I've blogged at www.cynthiaharrison.com.

Email me anytime at cindy@cynthiaharrison.com.

http://www.cynthiaharrison.com